£ 7-60

CH00685281

THE TENEMENT

THE TENEMENT

A NOVEL

by

IAIN CRICHTON SMITH

LONDON
VICTOR GOLLANCZ LTD
1985

First published in Great Britain 1985
by Victor Gollancz Ltd,
14 Henrietta Street, London WC2E 8QJ

British Library Cataloguing in Publication Data
Smith, Iain Crichton
    The tenement.
    I. Title
    823'.914 [F]   PR6005.R58
    ISBN 0-575-03669-9

Photoset and printed in Great Britain by
Photobooks (Bristol) Ltd

THE TENEMENT

THE TENEMENT WAS over a hundred years old. It faced the street with its grey granite stone, and its old windows which in order to be cleaned had to be manoeuvred on ropes like glassy sails, and its greenish door on which passing boys and men had scrawled graffiti. There were six flats in the tenement, some in good condition, some in bad: stone stairs led from floor to floor. Outside at the back was a maze of old pipes winding like rusty snakes: these usually suffered from bursts in the winter time, and there were arguments among the tenants about payment to the plumber.

The roof often needed repair, as water would come in on the tenants in the top flats. Four of the flats had been bought outright, two were rented. It was by no means the worst tenement in the street, for opposite it were worse ones, composed of cheap brick. In the latter, parties went on at weekends—there were rumours of prostitution—and on summer nights boys would sit on balconies shouting insults at the tourists or playing radios very loudly. Or they would emerge from the close on large black foreign bikes.

At night the tenants of the tenement would hear the shouts and songs of passing drunks, floating up from the street, as if magnified by the stone of the pavements or the walls. "I'll cut you up, you bastard," one voice would say, and another one, "Pass the f. . .ing bottle!" Quarrels would break out suddenly between those who had minutes before been friends. Girls and women would scream as if they had been knifed and there would be the drumming of running feet. The women's language was as bad as that of the men and they would be heard encouraging two fighters. "Put the f. . .ing boot in!" one would hear a girl scream in ecstasy. And the night was a time of preying, of quarrelling, of demented cries, as of shrill birds with bitter beaks.

The weather around the tenement changed. On spring days it was dry and clear, on summer days it was steamy and hot, on autumn days it was regretful and nostalgic, on winter days it was slushy and wet. And many different families over the years had seen that change in the weather, in the atmosphere, for there was considerable movement to and from the tenement. Wardrobes, sideboards with mirrors reflecting scarred white-washed walls, were carried upstairs and downstairs. Chairs and sofas were abandoned momentarily on a landing. Wallpaper was stripped and pasted on, ceilings were painted, there was a flowering of hope and a fading of it. Old ranges were removed, new fireplaces installed. Ancient bells that had wires, and tinkled in the kitchen, were replaced by push-button ones. A whole world was born, a whole world ceased. In one flat there might be a din of modern music, in another the sentimental tones of John MacCormack, in yet another no music at all.

And everywhere there was a sense of the past as if while one was sitting in the living room the door might open and a woman or man dressed in Edwardian clothes might enter. When one was, for instance, stripping wallpaper one might find a message written by newly weds eighty years before—JOHN AND AGNES SIGNED THIS. Or it might say, WILLIAM STEEL, CARPENTER. What days, what nights, what suns, what moons, had circled that tenement: what beds had produced what children, who had perhaps played on the stairs, on the diminutive green at the back of the tenement where the washing was hung out on windy days, a gallery of mended shirts and vests and blouses.

Some tenants had kept cats against the law, some had not. Some had been working men, some had been professional men just starting, for in later, more successful years they would move from the tenement. And yet, perhaps it left its mark on all of them, so that, in their later private houses or in the windy council schemes, they would always remember the period, long or short, that they had spent there.

One could not say that the coming together into that

tenement was anything other than a random action. The flats were like nests which happened to be beside each other, to which different birds came. It happened that two name-plates shone beside each other: there was nothing predestined about it. The inhabitants landed and left, and once they had left they might never see each other again. No roots were set down here as in villages, no stones echoed with remembered events, and the moon above it was not a local one. The curtains on the windows were of different colours, there were different coloured carpets on the floors, different ambitions inside the rooms. The flats existed differently in the minds of those who had left them and those who occupied them. Some remembered them with affection and some with loathing. Some could hardly believe that they had once lived there and, passing the building years later, in a car perhaps, would look up at the window of a room they had once occupied and feel an intense absence. Could they really have lived there? Surely not. Maybe they had inhabited different bodies then. They might even have an impulse to visit the flat again: where there had once been yellow armchairs there were now red ones, where once there had been an ancient bath as big as a stone grave, there was now a bathroom suite in warm colours.

The tenement survived all individuals who had inhabited it, the particulars which had been and gone. It survived the relentless blizzard of names, the ambitions, the despairs, the joys, the weddings, the funerals. It was like a soul which animates the body. Something of itself passed into the people who lived in it. Sweat leaked from the walls as if the tenement itself were perspiring. It sailed into the night and sailed back in the morning. With its eight windows facing the street it brooded over cars, pedestrians, the church opposite where the photographer knelt on a windy spring day as the bride's gown billowed outwards like a wave, as the shining black hearse moved slowly away with its crowns of flowers, as the minister stood meditatively near the gravestones in his black robe.

Beside it was a cafe that was open till eleven o'clock at night, in front of it was the church. Not far from it was the school, also built in grey granite. Its close was a mouth that swallowed, spat out. Its walls had graffiti on it almost as mysterious as Egyptian writing. Its bulging scarred green door had been painted years before. There was a window on the first landing which had white lacy curtains across it. The window on the second landing was uncurtained. The stairs were washed once a week. The landing lights were put on on alternate weeks by neighbouring tenants. For some trivial reason one tenant might not talk to another one, for weeks, for months, for years: every one of us has his own dignity, his own honour. It might be that one had used the other's bin without permission, or had forgotten his week for the light, or had heard the other talking behind his back. And these slights were burrs sticking in the heart, throbbing, feverish. For each one cries out, I am, I am, even in a tenement, perhaps especially in a tenement.

The building occupied space, occupied time. Around it other buildings had crumbled, risen, changed ownership. Its stone had been taken from a quarry that no longer existed. Its original masons, joiners, painters, were all dead. As Keats says that individual nightingales die though the generic nightingale doesn't, so each tenant would die but the tenement would seem to live for ever.

Sometimes the tenement could be imagined as a tree with transient nests in it, sometimes as composed of boxes that in turn held coffins, cradles, sometimes as a theatre where casts (actors and actresses) changed as they moved on to other plays. It might even be that the young ones were the old come back again in a different disguise or mask. The tenement in its transient solidity encouraged such speculations and baffled them by its enigmatic front. Windows too could be seen as eyes, fading, brightening. The door—what was it but the entrance to a fertile womb that bred incessantly? It was a prison door, it was a door for escaping through. It was a door which hid secrets, which released them to the world.

On spring days curtains, often white, fluttered at windows

like ghosts trying to get in or trying to get out, with frantic motions, with fragile winds.

Any story that can be told about one tenant has at best only a frail relationship to the story of another tenant but there will be some connection, however passing, however faint. And sometimes the tenants can act together, each having his own idea of what is happening, each taking a colour from the others, each merging briefly with the others like a cloud fading into a second one. So that the tenement itself can be seen not as made of stone but like a cloud that changes shape, merciful, cruel, wandering.

At the time of which we are speaking, there were no children in the tenement, maybe because most of the flats weren't large. Old people, mostly widowed, stayed in them, or young couples as yet without children. Perhaps the tenement was too old to put up with children, perhaps it didn't like them. Perhaps the tenement itself was drawing to its end, and had had in its day its complement of children which had left and never returned. Perhaps it hated ingratitude, random brilliance, wanted to settle down in its old age. Who can tell about a tenement? Maybe it said to couples with children, This is not the place for you; Go somewhere else. I have had enough of young ones, I have grown philosophical, children have no history, I can't learn from them. I only want those who have lived, not those who are about to live. I am a listener to stories that have happened, not stories that might happen years from now. And in any case I know that the children will live their lives out elsewhere, far from here, even if they stay for a brief time. My face is a Greek one, flat and incurious, like one of these blind stone faces that one sees in a garden wall in Greece. I have neither love nor hate, I am simply the stage on which things happen. And nothing of importance happens to children. And in any case that is all that life is, a passing show. I am not so stupid or so proud as to think that I am anything other than a habitation: I do not confer a meaning. Perhaps there is no meaning. Perhaps I am the only meaning there is. Perhaps I am a hundred meanings, a thousand. Perhaps I am a dementia of my tenants, a chimera. I am changed, plastered anew, and to all that I submit. Yet there is in me something that is always recognizable, that exists through all alterations, all neglect. And perhaps that memory will persist somewhere even when my stone has crumbled to dust, and perhaps passing on a certain day in summer or autumn someone will be struck by a thought that is not his own but is wafted from me. Is there anyone who knows? Or is all, mystery?

THE LIGHTNING HAD come out of the sky and had almost killed her but not quite. Jim, repairing the telephone wires, had been crucified on them in blue. When she was told about it she thought she would die, but she hadn't. They had three children, two girls and a boy, ranging from five years old to nine, the boy being the oldest. She used to be a waitress before her marriage, then she had the children, and now after Jim's crucifixion she went back to being a waitress again. When she returned to her old job she could hardly bear to think that there had been a time when she had stood carelessly at a table, notebook in hand, waiting to take down the order asked for, for example, soup, tomato, steaks, pudding. She couldn't believe that she had done that and now she could hardly do it without her heart breaking.

She had been very pretty and was now almost beautiful. The difference between being pretty and being beautiful is experience. It is perhaps a matter of suffering. One day she had rushed in to tell the chef that there was a smell of fire. "Where from?" he said, "I can't get it." And indeed there was no smell of fire at all. yet she had smelt the smoky stench, the scorching. That had happened the day after she had started again in the restaurant. It was more like a singeing, not a clean burning.

The children had saved her, and yet they were as selfish as other children. She had thought, Perhaps they will recognize my great love for their father and won't bother me so much. But they hadn't of course made any such recognition. They fought a great deal of the time, they shouted at each other, they envied each other, they accused her of favouritism. She did perhaps favour the boy more, because of Jim. And yet the boy too was selfish, he would ask her for money when there wasn't much, he would do sly things that would incriminate the girls, and then she didn't think he was like Jim at all. But perhaps Jim had done selfish things too: it was just that she couldn't remember them. Or chose not to.

She was eighty years old. She wore a fur coat summer and winter. She put lipstick on her lips and powder on her face. She stayed by herself in the top flat of the tenement. Her flat was a mess, there were yellowing newspapers on the floor, empty whisky bottles in the corridor, white plaster dropped from the ceiling like seagull shit. She stank though she didn't know it: she never had a bath because she couldn't afford an immerser. She didn't light the flat at night but lay there in the dark like a mole. She never read a book or a newspaper. And of course she never went to church, since God was quite clearly a being who unjustly despatched the lightning that had killed her innocent husband and crucified him on the wire.

Because she had been a good waitress the proprietor of the restaurant where she had worked—and of course he changed, and bequeathed her to another owner—allowed her to sit in the restaurant every day drinking perhaps three cups of coffee in that time. That was all she did, drink cups of coffee. Sometimes, so as not to finish a coffee too quickly, she would let it grow cold till a scum formed on it. Sometimes she would stare out at the sea, at the wasp-striped yachts that were anchored in the water, doing in the winter a crazy dance as she herself had done when she was young.

There had been, after she went back, widowed, men who had wanted to take her out, even marry her. There was the gardener who spent his time making words out of flowers and who complained of a bad back. He had never married but stayed by himself in a flat where he watched TV late into the night: before the advent of TV he used to go to the cinema three times a week; thus he had seen every film that ever came to the town. She didn't marry him, partly because of his complaints, and partly because he had begun to drink heavily. And also his breath, for that of a gardener, stank. He was not the only one who had tried to make up to her. There had been a janitor as well: he told her that he more or less ran the school and that he phoned the Director of Education regularly to give him the benefit of his advice: the Director called him Bill.

In fact, she never remarried and drank cups of coffee every day. Sometimes a man who lived in a cave outside the town came to the restaurant. He wore a rope for a belt to tie his long coat, was tall, and always clean shaven, except for his moustache which made him look like a brigand. The two of them talked a lot. On a lucky day they might go along to the draughty railway station and drink, or have a singsong along with other friends of theirs who staggered in and out of lavatories.

She didn't like most of the people in the tenement. For instance she hadn't liked the matron and she hadn't liked Mrs Brown, would never indeed like her, even though she was on the same landing. And she didn't like Mr and Mrs Porter either. Well, she liked Mrs Porter better than she liked Mr Porter, give her that. She thought the latter looked down on her, and he probably did. She would never let anyone into her own flat: she would rather have died. She was ashamed that it was so untidy. Every morning she meant to tidy it but she never did, she didn't have the energy. And yet she always made sure that she powdered and lipsticked herself before she went out. No one would believe she was eighty. No one.

One day a Health Visitor had knocked on her door. She was a young girl who carried a briefcase and who shone with the ardent hope of youth. Oh, how hopeful she looked, just like herself when she had started as a waitress all those years ago. And this young girl had said,

"I've been sent along, Mrs Miller. We were wondering if you needed any help."

"F. .k off," she told the young girl, and the latter had finally turned away with her fresh leather briefcase and they had sent no one else to replace her. After all, thought the old lady, she had her freedom, her rights, they were taking a liberty with her, you didn't have to let these people in if you didn't want to, they couldn't force themselves on you. She sometimes saw the young Health Visitor around the town but the girl always turned her face away. She didn't have anything against her, it was only that she disliked the system that could send someone along to investigate you when you didn't want to be investigated. In fact she would have gone along to speak to her, to say that she was sorry, only that she was frightened that the girl would take the apology as a weakness, and visit her again, an opening of a closed door that would forever remain shut since that blue lightning flash.

She wouldn't let even her own son into the flat. He stayed in Helensburgh and though he was lame would sometimes visit her, having remembered about her. He was of course married, but his wife never came with him. She would meet him at the restaurant and on such days they would have a meal there and not simply a coffee. She had seen his nose twitch once or twice, and he had told her quite often, though not with great conviction, "You must come and stay with us." But she didn't want to go and stay with him as she didn't like her daughter-in-law who was a stuck-up bitch, to say the least of it, with a colour television set, a washing machine, a drier, a toaster, and all the other machines you could name. In fact she didn't like her son much either. He allowed himself to be dominated by his wife; she thought that no man should let that happen. Jim would never have allowed that to happen with her. She had never even tried to dominate him. He would go for his drink in the pub after work and she accepted that as being the normal thing. Her son Hugh never did that, he came home straight from his work, and he was never allowed to go for a drink on his own. And also he didn't really want her to come and stay with them. She knew that: one could tell a great deal from people's voices.

After they had had their lunch he would return to Helensburgh on the train. She would wave to him and he would wave to her and if he left her money she would go and have a drink in the station buffet—where she would meet Kansas Mary, though who gave her that name she didn't know—and the Brigand: and they would sing songs with their arms around each other, and sometimes they might be reported to the police by the woman who ran the station bookstall who didn't like their swearing. It was strange and sad to think of her son going further and further away from her on a train to leafy Helensburgh, which she hated with a deadly hatred, because she had been in his house a few times and her daughter-in-law had asked her whether she had a colour TV or whether she had a washing machine (sniffing around her fur coat and generally speaking trying to make her feel inferior, which she didn't do, couldn't manage to do). Anyway she considered her daughter-in-law to be ugly which she herself had never been, and she knew for a fact that the younger woman mostly bought her clothes cheap, much as she tried to act the big lady.

You don't know anything, she would mutter under her breath so that her daughter-in-law wouldn't hear her. What did they teach you in a girls' school anyway?

Actually, she didn't like Mr Porter at all though she was fairly fond of Mrs Porter. Mrs Porter often took her in for a coffee, had offered tactfully to clean the house out for her, but of course she didn't want that. So she stopped taking her coffee and anyway Mrs Porter was dead now. The husband, a teacher (retired) she wasn't greatly taken with, he was a bit snooty, like her daughter-in-law, and he never had much to say for himself. He would stand with his briefcase in his hand, not able to make any conversation. He was bald on top with grey hair round the edge of the baldness, and he always wore a crushed hat.

Once Mrs Porter had given her her Christmas dinner and of course she had lipsticked and powdered herself more than usual. She had even bought a bottle of cheap wine. Looking in the mirror, she could swear that no one would take her for eighty. They had a beautiful dinner: and crackers which they opened. She got a toy car and she wore the the tall paper hat on top of her head all during the dinner. It was soup to start with, then duck, then trifle. Mrs Porter also had Drambuie and After-Eights. She knew how to handle herself, she knew about crackers, about food, the right spoons and forks and knives, and she knew about drink. They watched television (colour) all day and she didn't want to leave, she was so warm. Even Mr Porter had tried to make conversation with her, in his own odd jerky way. He would ask her about the changes in the town and she was able to tell him that where the Chapel of Ease had once been there was now a warehouse, and where MacDonald's had once been there was now a post office.

Conversation somehow got round to Macmillan who used to wander around the town singing and frothing at the mouth. He drank anything, meths, furniture polish, Brasso, and he sang opera, marching like a regular soldier. She told them that the story she had heard was that a big yacht had once anchored in the town and Macmillan had fallen in love with one of the upper-class girls on it (at that time he had been a handsome man who had a career as a singer ahead of him). Then the girl had jilted him and sailed away in the big white yacht and he had taken to drinking and had never stopped since. Now of course he was in a drying-out place in Glasgow. But he was still alive, he must have had an iron stomach. Mr Porter had been interested in that story as it was said that he was a poet and sometimes got letters from Spain and Portugal and so on. She herself never got any letters except bills which she immediately rolled up and threw away. Even at Christmas time she didn't put the electric light or the heater on, though the Porters always had a Christmas tree. It was said that it was Mrs Porter who put it up.

Mrs Porter had told her not to tell Mr Porter that the two of them sometimes had coffee together. Was it because Mr Porter didn't think she was good enough to talk to his wife? And then sometimes Mrs Porter would slip a pound note into her hand. "Don't tell anyone," she would say. Of course she spent it all on drink though that wasn't what Mrs Porter had given her the money for.

There was a film on that Christmas Day called *The Guns of Navarone*. She liked it and she liked the Queen's speech. She liked

Morecambe and Wise as well. All that didn't explain what happened the following day, even after Mrs Porter had left a piece of cake, which she had made herself, in a packet outside her door. Nothing explained what happened the following day: it was her shame and yet at the time it felt natural, imperative. Or at least she had thought and felt so. Nowadays she didn't give a damn for anyone. Since God's justice had failed her what could she expect from man? It might even be that it gave the Porters a kick to give her her Christmas dinner and expect that forever afterwards she would bow down to them. Mrs Porter had taken her secretly aside and said, "I will clean your flat. Not even my husband will know." What was bothering her of course was the contrast between the clean waitress she had been and the tramp she had become, without energy, without shame. How could Mrs Porter know anything about that?

What had happened was quite simple. After she had spent all Christmas Day in the Porter flat, after she had eaten their soup, their duck, their trifle, their cake, and drunk their wine, after she had watched the programmes on colour television, after she had enjoyed herself and had then climbed the stairs into her cold dark uncomfortable flat, thinking of her husband crucified in blue and twitching in the light, the following day she had met Mrs Porter on the stair and she hadn't spoken to Mrs Porter at all. She had walked past her as if she wasn't there. Now, wasn't that odd? What could one make of that? Anyway, Mrs Porter had looked quite shocked and had never asked her in for coffee again. But why had she done it, why had she ignored Mrs Porter? That was what she couldn't understand. In her youth she would never have been so rude. But now she felt bitter, really bitter; not even colour TV could cure her ills. That day she had got murderously drunk and had staggered up the stair meeting Mrs Porter on the way, who had almost lifted her skirt delicately aside. Why, she could remember practically crawling on her hands and knees looking up like a suppliant whose heart is full of evil at the stunned red face. Mean bitch, she wouldn't give her pee to the cat.

*

She had crawled past the flat of the Masons who had complained to her when she had come home from Rhodesia after visiting her daughter. They had said that while she was away she had left her water on and it had poured down through the ceiling and ruined their new wallpaper. That was the kind of welcome to which she had come back: imagine it. She had been so happy, too, after a glorious six months' holiday with her daughter: and the blacks had called her 'mamma' and she had sat in the garden drinking soft drinks and sometimes strong ones while the eternal sunlight shone blandly on her. Her daughter and her husband had taken her to see the Falls, and she had shopped in Salisbury. Of course she had heard horrifying stories, like that of the farmer whose head had been cut off and hung on the branch of a tree by the guerrillas so that his wife could see his grey moustache in the clear day. She herself agreed with her daughter. The blacks were really stupid and ungrateful, you couldn't bequeath a country to them. Absurd to think you could. And that fellow Mugabe was like a dwarf: and she heard an anecdote about a black leader who had been given cheese wrapped in silver paper and had eaten the silver paper too. The blacks were backward, of course they were, and treacherous too after all the whites had done for them.

Carol and Tom treated them well, why, they would even give them some of the left-over meat, but still you could never be sure with them, they smiled so widely, showing white teeth, but who knew their real thoughts? But they hadn't harmed her, they smiled, and laughed with her. The Falls had been spectacular, all that water pouring down in the brightness of the day. They had seen some wild life too and Tom used to fish for tiger fish. Of course you didn't eat tiger fish, well maybe the blacks did, the struggle with the tiger fish was only for the sake of the sport, it was part of the game of life that had made the whites great. At least this was what Tom would say standing there in his shorts, like a schoolboy, showing his knobbly knees.

Oh, Carol had told her to stay longer, but of course she

hadn't, because Carol hadn't really meant it. After all, she had two sons and a daughter: the son was a fine sportsman and doing well in his school. Every Christmas instead of a card Carol would send a photograph of the kids, who were calm and well-behaved. Very polite all the kids were, but quite distant too, they'd never had to do anything; Carol too didn't have to do anything, the blacks did all the cooking. She doubted whether Carol's daughter could boil an egg. The kids so remote and spoiled already, though it was right that the blacks should be the servants, they were born to be servants, even though they were quite stupid and couldn't even take a telephone message correctly.

Tom played golf a lot and in the evening there would be visitors and they would have drinks. They drank quite a lot, there wasn't much else to do; and the schools, too, she noticed, started earlier than in Scotland because of the heat. But she didn't mind the heat: there you spent money on electricity to keep cool, here you spent money on electricity in order to keep warm. She loved the heat, she had never been so happy, and she had reminded Carol of events in the days of her youth, as when for example Carol had come in drunk one night at the age of seventeen (still in school, in fact) and she herself poured a bucketful of cold water over her in the bath and Carol had said spluttering, "You're a pal, mum." She reminded her of many incidents but they never talked about Jim, crucified on the wires. He had been a post office engineer, a good one too.

The shock had hit her heart that night and she had never recovered. You never did, no matter what people said. She remembered that after his death the couple below her, the Willises, had asked her for a loan of her stepladder as they were painting their ceilings, and she wouldn't give it to them. And this in spite of the fact that they knew she had the stepladder and she knew that they knew. Mr Willis, who was a young policeman, had been very hurt. But she didn't want to give them the ladder: she didn't want to give them anything, they were the lucky ones: they hadn't been struck out of the sky. God was on their side.

The day she had boarded the plane returning from Rhodesia she had met a man from Dundee whom she had also seen on the way out. He was about sixty and both times he was drunk. He had confided in her that he was frightened of planes. He had sat at the back, and the next thing there was an awful stramash. He had staggered to the lavatory and was busily engaged in trying to tug open the Emergency Door, which he thought was the door to the toilet, when he had been dragged away by a steward. He had then been placed between two big stalwart passengers for the rest of the flight. If he had succeeded in opening that door he would have blown them to Kingdom Come.

Oh, she had loved Rhodesia. Never again would she find a place that she liked so much. It was ideal for servants. Only their television wasn't very good. It consisted of political speeches by self-important black men. Mugabe always looked tense and arrogant. The bishop was better than him, at least he was dressed in a nicer way. And the big jovial man at least showed he had some life in him: she liked him best of all. No, she would never find a place like that again, though Carol was saying that they would have to leave and they would only be able to take a thousand pounds with them. And they would lose their house and their swimming pool and God knew what would happen to the children, as Carol had hoped to send them to college or university.

And then she had come home to the complaint from the Masons; really it was wicked of them. She had been so pleased with her photographs and her gifts, and she was so sunburnt and she had never felt so well in her life, and she had so many stories and they had to spoil it all with news of their crumby flat and their stained wallpaper. Imagine coming down to these ratty flats with their squalid problems when she had flown home from Rhodesia! And in any case they didn't realize that her own flat had been flooded by water: they never thought of that. She had left the carpet as it was, to dry as best it could, and that was the

beginning of the neglect. The day of her homecoming she had
sat on the bed and cried. And the Masons wouldn't speak to her
when they met her on the stair. Oh, the tenement looked rotten
and rat-ridden though it really wasn't, but in comparison with the
big airy house in Rhodesia it did: she had brought back
photographs of it, with the verandah and the beautiful trees and
the lovely car they had just outside the garage and Tom waving
through the open window of it.

Oh, she had suffered. What did they care about Jim and the
crucifixion? Nothing. No one remembered what she had been
like when young, how efficient she had been. Why, the owner
had wanted to make her a manageress but she wouldn't take the
job as the children were growing up and she didn't know
whether she could cope or not. Anyway the children were away
now and she was alone.

The Brigand had asked her to come and stay with him in the
cave. But she didn't want that though the Brigand said that you
could get used to it. The cave was along the shore a bit, and she
had been there once with him and they had drunk a whole bottle
of whisky. He even had candles in the depths of the cave but she
couldn't imagine what it would be like in the winter. They said
that the Brigand's father was a professor and he had run away
from home years before, but you could never tell, there were so
many stories, as with Macmillan. Perhaps in his case there
hadn't been a girl at all, or a yacht, and the tale had been made
up. But when there was no one else to talk to there was always
the Brigand. In the olden days she would never even have
glanced at him, she would have been horrified to hear of anyone
living in a cave. Macmillan had done that too and he would go
round the hotels collecting empty bottles to sell for a few
pennies. If you gave him any money he wouldn't leave you alone
but marched behind you step for step all day as if he were
imitating you, mocking you, barking military orders while at
the same time singing snatches of Italian opera in the original.
There was always a thin rim of froth round his lips.

"You were quite right not to let that girl in," said the Brigand in his polite English accent. "They have no right to come and impose themselves on you."

"You're dead right. The liberty," she said, her nostrils flaring. Though the girl had been nice: it wasn't her fault. But she would rather lie stretched on the floor than let anyone from the Health Department come and see her. They hadn't helped her when she had needed them most. Now they could go to hell and back in a chariot if they wanted to. Where were they when she had the fainting spells? In those days she would sometimes faint while carrying a tray over to a table. The proprietor had been very good, he had allowed her to carry on and eventually the fainting spells had stopped, though they had been bad while they lasted. And migraines too. Awful pains which lit up her face, sparked in front of her eyes. Nothing would cure the pain till the sickness came.

Now there was Mr Cooper in the bottom flat opposite the Masons (who had put in for the flat below when the nurse had died): and his wife had passed away but he seemed to get over it. Mr Porter too had lost his wife but he acted funny: he had been funny most of his life if you were to ask her. Now the Masons had left the middle flat it was Mrs Floss who stayed there. Mrs Floss was always changing the furniture in her flat: she had plenty of money, her husband had owned an hotel. Mrs Brown who had stayed next to herself on the top flat had died too. When she was alive she used to take a taxi out to the cemetery to visit the grave of her husband. She herself never went to Jim's grave, she couldn't bear to. That day she had cried so much (the day of the funeral), and there had been a lot of flowers and wreaths, for Jim had been very popular and obliging, but she had never gone to see the grave again. It was as if his body wasn't really there, as if it had melted in the lightning. She didn't believe in God, she didn't believe that Jim would live again, that she would ever see him again, all that talk was crap: you had your life on this earth, you were lucky or not, that was what it all came down to. Mrs Floss below her often mentioned souls passing from body to body, reincarnation she called it, but she didn't believe that either. Of course since Mrs Floss had lost her husband she had been away on a number of world cruises, she had tons of money, but she had odd ideas. And to see her in the summer in a bikini stretched out on a deckchair on the back green was a sight that one would never forget. She looked like a stranded whale. It almost made you cry laughing. Die laughing.

Carol didn't believe in God either. If God was good he wouldn't give this country to the blacks, she would say. Even He must know how stupid they were. If it was left to them the country would be a mess, chaotic, ungovernable, dirty. And she herself believed that. They would never have cultivated the country, tilled the land, you could see they were incapable of it, all they wanted was bicycles and cars. And they would sleep all day in the sun if they were allowed to. Their minds were so primitive and illogical. One day a black servant had come to Carol and said he was leaving. "Why?" she had asked him. "You have just been given a raise." "It's because of that I'm leaving," he had told her. "Because of the raise?" "Yes, you've been cheating me; if I was worth that money, I should have been given it from the beginning." How they reasoned was beyond one's understanding, Carol would say.

She herself had been given a raise by the restaurant manager. "Because you are a nice efficient girl with a pleasant manner," he told her. "Because you are conscientious," smiling through his pencil-thin moustache. Of course he had fancied her but she hadn't fancied him. He had tried to make her, but she took the raise and kept out of his way as much as possible. Then he had been caught cooking the books because he was keeping a mistress and she hadn't seen him again. Over sexed he had been but a good manager too: the over sexed ones always made the best managers. He let you get on with your job but he had that eye. Of course since Jim, there would be no one for her. Not like that.

She had even thought of joining the Catholic Church. They helped each other in their trouble. What had happened was that a young girl who had started as a waitress in the restaurant had a baby and the baby died. The baby had been in an incubator for five days and had faded gently away while being taken to the big Children's Hospital in Glasgow in an ambulance: its heart had given out. Anyway the girl had been heartbroken but the priest had been magnificent. He had told her that the baby was an angel in heaven and the girl had such faith that she believed him and was comforted. They had buried the baby in a coffin the size of a shoe box and they had baptized it before that. The Protestants believed that you began in sin, and continued in sin. So she had nearly joined the Catholic Church and she had even gone to hear one of their services in the Cathedral by the sea where there was a crib and the Virgin Mary holding the Child Jesus in her arms. And the girl had said to her, "One night, I went to the Cathedral and I saw the Virgin Mary holding the baby out and it seemed that she was offering it to me instead of my own. And that was when I got better." She too had a Health Visitor come to see her and the Health Visitor had said, "Don't keep that photograph of your baby in front of you all the time" (the photograph had been taken while the baby was in the incubator and you couldn't approach too closely in case you imported human germs to it). But the girl hadn't shifted the photograph from where it was and the Health Visitor never referred to it again.

Winter nights were the worst. It was so cold in the flat. And sometimes she would think that Jim was there. One day just after his death, the kids being in school and she herself coming into the house during the dinner hour, she had heard someone talking in the flat. She opened all the doors but still the talking went on, though no one could be seen. It was a man's voice too, quite low, and she thought, My God, Jim has come back from the dead. But it wasn't that at all. It was in fact the radio that she must have forgotten to switch off in the morning, though she had turned it down, and the voice was coming from that. It had given her a terrible shock. Maybe one of the girls had left it on. They were always leaving things on, lights, radios, television.

Anyway she was quite happy in the restaurant, drinking her coffee. And she would watch the sea, or the people passing on the road. There was always something to be seen. Once, there had been a huge storm, and seaweed strewn all over the road, and in the shops. Tree trunks had been torn out of the ground, the sea-wall had been twisted as if by a giant hand.

And she would sometimes think about the people in the flats. Mrs Brown, who had used to take the flowers to her husband's grave, had been so mean that she wouldn't even buy the local paper. She herself had to lend her her own copy, but now she had stopped buying it. When Jim was alive she would say, "Poor woman. She's got nobody. I don't mind lending the paper." But she wouldn't say that now.

"My God," he would say, "she doesn't deserve to have anybody visit her. She's got plenty of money and she won't spend it. She uses our bin sometimes." Which of course she did and had put empty bottles of sherry in it though she claimed that she didn't drink.

Always sniffing about with a brush in her hand cleaning the stair as if no one did it but herself. The queen of the tenement. And so meek and mild too with her face coloured red from the blood pressure. Always picking up bits of paper as if they were treasure trove and saying that people should stick to their own day for the washing. And doing a bit of weeding since no one else bothered about the back green. When they had visited her house on the day of her death they had found all the rooms tightly crowded with furniture, like a second-hand shop. It was as if she had been building a fortress to keep the world out. And yet her house was spotless though crowded, with a smell of Mansion Polish.

So that was herself, now, who stayed in a top flat, with Mr and Mrs Cameron on the same landing: and below her was Mrs Floss and beside her was Mr and Mrs Porter: and below them was Mr Cooper and beside him were the Masons, the ones who had complained about their stained wallpaper.

She'd better remember: fix it all in her mind.

27

Mrs Miller	Mr and Mrs Cameron
Mrs Floss	Mr and Mrs Porter
Mr and Mrs Mason	Mr Cooper

She had noticed for a while the two young people who came into the restaurant and often sat at the table next to her. One was a tall boy of about seventeen who wore school uniform of a navy blue colour with yellow edgings on the jacket. She thought he was a prefect. (Neither of her own children had been prefects.) With him was his girl friend who was almost as tall as himself, wearing the same colour of uniform. They would come in at lunchtime and sit opposite each other holding hands and gazing into each other's eyes. The boy always came in first and then the girl. And they talked a lot. What did they find to talk about? Stories about school probably. They never spoke to her but she imagined that they would notice her, wonder about her. In their presence she felt more lonely than ever. They reminded her of her own children but they were more polite, perhaps the son and daughter of professional people.

For much of the time she pretended that she didn't see them and stared out of the window at the sea where a tinker piper often played to the tourists in his ragged tartan. When the tide was out there were papers and plastic cups to be seen lying on the shore. When the tide was in the sea rose to the horizon, silver and glittering, and sometimes one could watch big ships passing. The winter days were long and dark. In the summer time, however, there was much to see. There were so many tourists from so many different countries, wearing the national dress: Indians in saris, Americans in white jackets, and white hats, just as in *Dallas*. The place in the summer seemed to blossom, become alive. It was a smallish town of perhaps ten thousand people. In the summer, however, it was increased to about twenty thousand.

In the summer, too, the scholars seemed happy and fresh and

radiant. It was as if they were full of hope, their whole lives ahead of them. They were absorbed in each other though this didn't mean that they didn't quarrel at times. She could tell when they had quarrelled. The boy would come in earlier than usual and he would wait, glancing at his watch and fidgeting and sometimes whistling, and pretending that he was not waiting for the girl at all. Once he had left before she arrived.

But their quarrels were only occasional. Usually they held a continuous conversation. She could hear snatches of what they were talking about, for instance a remark about Old Spotty, who, she assumed, must be a teacher. Then they would discuss their examinations. The girl, she gathered, wasn't good at maths and might not be able to go to the same university as the boy who, she thought, was cleverer. They discussed their maths teacher a lot. He was violent, bad-tempered, and oppressive, and frightened his pupils so much that they couldn't concentrate on their work. The school was their whole world. Once the maths teacher had thrown a Bible at someone, for she gathered that he taught Religious Education to his register class. He had wakened out of a sleep and thrown his Bible at a girl who was sitting at the back of the class dreaming. The Bible had shot past her head and rebounded from the wall.

The girl was tall and had corn-coloured hair. The boy was dark-haired, handsome and, she thought, athletic. The girl wore a ring on her finger. It might not be an official engagement ring but would serve as one. Sometimes if she was in a bad mood she would turn the ring over and over. On such days the ring seemed to inflame her finger and this told her, according to herself, something about the boy's faithfulness or lack of it. "Rubbish," the boy would say, "all that is psychological."

"No, it's not," the girl would say. She always took an *Express* in with her and they compared horoscopes. She could tell that the girl believed in them but that the boy didn't. The girl was a Pisces and the boy an Aquarius.

She had heard the boy say once, "How can everybody born under Pisces have the same fortune for a particular day? And

29

then if you buy a *Mirror* or a *Sun* it will give you a different horoscope." The girl then became technical saying that she might not be wholly a Pisces or he wholly an Aquarius. It depended on the exact hour at which you were born. She herself had been born at two in the morning: the boy didn't know the exact hour of his birth.

The old woman sipped her coffee. Sometimes scum formed on it. She would look out at the street and say to herself, "Imagine any woman wearing a hat like that! And really, that boy who has just passed with green hair!" They would do anything to draw attention to themselves. Some of them looked like Red Indians and some had no hair at all. She had once made a mistake with that Catholic girl, telling her that there was a spot of dirt on her brow. In actual fact the spot was associated with a particular Catholic date, Ash Wednesday. The girl hadn't been offended at all.

She felt awfully sweaty and now and again scratched herself. She often had bad constipation and her eyesight was not as good as it had been. But she wore her fur coat all the time, she even slept in it. She often felt like an animal in a pelt.

One day the boy and the girl had an awful row. It was to do with a girl called Joan. This Joan, as far as she could make out, had joined the magazine committee on which the boy was editor. Joan had been trying to make up to him and had gone round the school with him putting up posters to advertise the magazine.

"You were with her. You were seen," the girl hissed.

"Who saw me?"

"Sheila for one. She told me."

"Sheila's a cross-eyed bitch."

"She's not cross-eyed even though she wears glasses."

"What can I do? I have to go around the school putting up advertisements: otherwise no one would buy the magazine. It was Scruffy who told me to do it. I couldn't turn round and say to her, 'You can't come'. Anyway she can write quite well."

"Quite well? Who told you that?"

"I know it. I've seen some of her stuff. That's why she's on the committee."

"It's not. It's because Scruffy likes her. Anyway there were others you could have gone around with."

"It was Scruffy who sent us. I just told you."

"That's what you say. You were talking to her all the time, laughing and joking."

"What am I supposed to do? Not speak to her? Be reasonable. She's on the same committee."

"It's you who's not being reasonable. It doesn't have to be a girl you go round with: does it?"

"She's pretty competent actually. I'm not saying that because I'm in love with her or anything. But she is. And she does work, more than most of them. Some of the people on the committee just treat it as a skive."

"We know why she works for you. The other girls don't like her. She's a clype."

And so on and so on. The quarrel went for ages. Periodically through the summer it flared up and died down again like an inflammation on a finger. Sometimes the girl would be deliberately late. Sometimes the boy would sit silently glaring at her with compressed lips. Sometimes the girl would refuse to take her coffee or the boy would.

Then a wholly different quarrel started. This one had to do with a play which the girl was taking part in, and of which the boy disapproved. It was clear that the only reason that the girl had joined the drama group was to get her own back on the boy.

"You don't have to get a lift home with him," the boy would say, and the girl would answer, "What else can I do?"

"You needn't have been in the play at all."

"*You* needn't have been on the magazine committee."

"That's different."

"How is it different?"

"It is. It's pretty obvious to anyone why it's different."

"What do you mean to anyone! Are you implying that I'm stupid or something?"

31

"You know perfectly well I've been editing the magazine for two years. You've never acted in a play before. You've never shown any interest."

"Well, I've to start sometime."

It seemed that another boy called Slim who apparently was a brilliant actor ran her home in his father's car after the rehearsals. Slim was the son of a local doctor, played rugby, had a lot of pocket money, sometimes drank, was also a prefect. It was obvious that he was a formidable rival.

At times as she watched the two of them the old lady would see herself bending down to take an order from a customer. She too had blonde hair though she wasn't as tall as the girl. It was as if that picture were superimposed on the one she saw in front of her. Or it might be that she saw Jim coming in the door after his work and they would talk animatedly and she would bring him a cup of tea which he didn't have to pay for.

Now, however, when she saw him there was a scar from the lightning snaking across his brow.

As a matter of fact, she hated the boy and the girl. She hated them not simply because they were young, not even because they quarrelled. At least a quarrel was a sign of life. It was better to quarrel than to be silent, fuming and fretting. She considered them, however, silly. Imagine having quarrels about such silly things. In fact she found it hard to explain to herself what her feelings about them were. Certainly there was envy and dislike, but there was something deeper than that. It was as if she saw in them her indifferent negligent children. But more than anything she hated them because they had a life ahead of them, a future ahead, and their days were populated with characters.

Of course after their quarrels they would make up and gaze into each other's eyes again. The boy would hold the girl's hand in his and stroke it gently. His soul was in his eyes. It was evident that this was the girl he loved, would always love, and that life would be good to them. The old woman wished that she could stare into the future and watch what happened. Did they in fact marry? Did they go to the same university? Did they have children? Were they safe from the crooked lightning?

And then one day they had the most tremendous quarrel and the girl threw the ring on the floor and stalked out. The boy ran after her without thinking about the ring. It rolled under the old lady's table and rested beside her shoe. She felt it almost burn her foot, sting it. She placed her shoe over it. Then making sure that no one saw her, she bent down and slipped it into her handbag, dropping a spoon on the floor first. She sat there staring out at the sea as if she had done something dramatic, novel, startling. Her heart was beating very fast.

And then the girl came in in a great hurry. She began immediately to search for the ring on the floor, but couldn't find it. She hesitated and finally came over to the old lady.

"Excuse me," she said, "did you see a ring on the floor?"

"No," said the old lady adamantly.

"Are you sure? I mean . . . It's just . . ." And she blushed. "It fell off my finger. You see it's very loose. Are you sure you haven't seen it?"

Suddenly the old lady said, "Are you accusing me of stealing it or what? I f. . .ing didn't see it."

The girl blushed and moved away.

However, the manager heard her swearing and came to inquire what had happened, standing there like Peacock in *Are you being served?*.

"She's f. . .ing accusing me of stealing her ring. I don't know about her ring." The old lady was furious.

"Keep your voice down," said the manager, glancing around him at the other customers in the restaurant.

"I won't keep my f. . .ing voice down," said the old lady. She was angry with the girl and also with the manager. She had never been a thief in her life. All the years of being allowed to drink coffee in the restaurant wounded her.

"I won't keep my f. . .ing voice down," she shouted.

"In that case you had better leave," said the manager.

She was so angry that she didn't care about the future. The girl was shifting from foot to foot not knowing what was happening and wanting to leave. Well, she could face reality for once, the upper class bitch, thought the old woman.

She ran out of the restaurant clutching her worn handbag, and shouting at the manager. She crossed the street and stood staring into the water, simmering. She didn't care what would happen to her now that she had got that off her chest. All her life she had been bowing and scraping to people, taking their orders, and she was fed up to the teeth. It was high time that she told the manager what she thought of him.

And that girl, tall and invulnerable in her uniform. She looked across at the restaurant from the other side of the street. It said, RONAL M ORE, B KER ND C NFECTI NER. The manager and the girl were bending down looking for the ring but they couldn't find it. Now they were talking to some of the other customers. The girl clearly couldn't understand why the ring wasn't on the floor. It was a magical disappearance. Perhaps she feared that love would disappear as inexplicably as the ring had done. But let her learn. Let her learn that disaster could strike out of the blue. Let her learn that the stars couldn't protect her. In fact the day her husband had been killed her own horoscope had said, "Good day for all practical purposes though it can be a dull one if you are bent on pleasure. So be more enterprising in seeking entertainment."

She walked away from the restaurant in the direction of the railway station. Some of her friends would be there drinking. It was as if she had severed connection with her usual world. Now she would not be able to go back to the restaurant. She knew what the manager was like, mean-minded, formal. She had seen many like him in the past. He had the same kind of walk as pompous Captain Peacock.

She thought at first of throwing the ring into the sea, imagining it dropping into the water, circling, spinning and falling, till it reached the bottom. Spinning in blue. The water near the shore was clear, transparent, and had a greenish tinge. She looked at the seagulls squabbling in a circle. Once she had seen a crab, another time an eel, white and upright in the water like a ghost. The fishing boats were anchored chastely, each showing the reflection of its name in the sea—*Sea Wanderer, Tern,* and so on.

On second thoughts she wouldn't throw the ring into the water at all. That would be a waste. The best thing would be to take it into a jeweller and sell it. In fact that's what she would do. After she had sold it she would buy a bottle of wine and drink herself stupid. She felt free as if she had emerged from a long servitude, as if she had broken though a necessary horizon.

She and the others would have a singsong in the station. And they would watch the trains leaving. In fact it looked as if in future she would have to take her coffee in the station buffet, though she didn't much like it. Too many tramps came into it. And there was a juke box which she didn't like.

She walked into the jeweller's having first taken the ring from her handbag. She had already forgotten about the girl and the boy. For the moment she had even forgotten about Jim. His hands were not held out to her. Horoscopes were a lot of f. . .ing rubbish, that was for sure. And as for that manager, he could stuff himself.

AFTER HIS WIFE died, Trevor Porter felt desolated. Whenever he picked up a handkerchief of hers he would weep like a child. Her presence seemed to be everywhere in the house even though her physical body no longer was. She had left everything tidy for him, the brooms and buckets in one cupboard, the food tins arranged and tabulated in another, and as far as that went he knew exactly where he was. But it was the explosion of herself from ordinary objects that bothered him most of all.

All his life he had been a teacher, sometimes in England, sometimes in Scotland. He hadn't been a good teacher. He had started just before the war, and during the war itself had served in the Navy mostly on convoys with icy decks heading for Russia with supplies. Even now he had nightmares about these times. He woke snorting from black seas that rolled over his head. Waiting under the water were enemies to trap him.

He had started teaching when English heads of department demanded that he inculcate ideas such as general analysis and figures of speech into youths who walked through Clydeside on grey mornings. When had they ever met an example of synecdoche or metonymy? Trevor had once mentioned to his chief that he felt that the curriculum was inept, absurd.

"We have to educate them out of their environment," the man, whose name was Trivett, had said.

"But they're not Greeks or mediaevalists," Trevor maintained. "They don't count the angels on the point of a needle."

"They will have to learn to write good English," said Trivett angrily. He had composed the curriculum himself. It was his only creative contribution to English Studies and he was rather proud of it.

Trevor spent some of his time in London teaching, among

others, Arabs and Jews, and Cypriots. He was interested in puns at that time, describing a fight between an Arab and a Jewish boy, and saying that the Arab had turned the other sheikh. These puns he thought funny, perhaps because he was a poet, but no one else did. Once he had found in the store a large consignment of the poetry of Dorothy Hemans. There was also an anthology called *Laurel and Gold*, which he called Laurel and Hardy. He felt that he was always having to teach texts that he could summon up no interest in.

As well as teaching in London he taught in Newark, Robin Hood country. One day walking with Julia in a wood he had said to her, "I don't think I can stay here much longer. They have asked me to produce plays. I can't produce plays."

"But it's a good school," said Julia.

"I know that," he said, "but I can't produce plays."

"You can't have everything," she said, through the dapple of shadows. "After all, the pupils are well behaved. Do you want well behaved pupils and perhaps more work to do, or do you want badly behaved pupils and finish at four?"

"I don't know," he said. "I can't produce plays. Nor do I like supervising cricket."

Julia was silent. Her whole life had been spent in packing, leaving one school and going on to another. She herself had been a school secretary when she met Trevor. She originally came from Devon, but he had met her in Glasgow.

She knew that her husband was a failure as a teacher though it was said he was a good poet. Even in London after the war he would send some of his poems home to Scotland to be published. She had once found a love poem that he had written to a sixth form girl but had never mentioned it to him.

In any case they had left Newark and had gone to Glasgow. Now they were in this smallish town to which they had retired. Above them lived the Camerons, beside them Mrs Floss. Mr Cameron beat his wife up regularly. There were hideous screams and screeches on Saturday nights, and then silence.

Often and often Trevor had made up his mind he would go upstairs and have it out with Cameron, but he never had the nerve. He thought that Mr Cameron would think up unimaginable methods of torment for him later, become much more evil, bang on the ceiling all night with a broom handle. He was quite capable of it. Sober he was fine, drunk he was intolerable.

Julia had wanted him to leave but he couldn't be bothered to shift any more. He was tired of shifting, and eventually she had acquiesced. So that they had to endure the Camerons. Trevor believed that it was Cameron with his din who had killed his wife. She had died of cancer.

One day shortly after Julia died the minister came to see him. He was a stooped man who looked like a superannuated scholar and who rode a bicycle.

"We have to endure what God sends us," he said. "Your wife used to do the flowers. She asked me to put up a prayer for you if anything happened to her."

"Oh," said Trevor.

"We never know the day nor the hour," said the minister. "She was sometimes embarrassed because she didn't have a proper garden. I think she would have liked a garden. And then again she often talked of Devon."

You old bastard, thought Trevor. You ancient hypocrite. He offered tea and biscuits which the minister had taken.

"It's an awful thing," said the minister, "but women compete about the flowers and even the playing of the organ." The last time Trevor had been in church he had thought that the organ pipes looked like atomic missiles laid end to end. As the minister inveighed against nuclear warfare, he had stroked back a stray curl.

"I hope you're managing," he said to Trevor.

"Yes," said Trevor. In fact he was inordinately practical for a poet. It was he who had wired the whole flat having lifted up the floorboards first before the carpets had been put down. He had also torn out a black range and put in a tiled fireplace. But of course he was absent-minded about his clothes. He wore a crushed hat always, and the same blue suit, shiny from use. Julia had long given up advising him on his dress.

Shortly before she died she looked for something. He found her wandering about the flat in her nightgown at three in the morning. But whatever she was searching for she stopped doing so when she saw that he was staring at her palely from the bars of red and white pyjamas.

He watched the TV. Boycott hadn't scored for an hour. The cat which he had found at the bins one morning, and which he had adopted, was sitting blinking on the window sill. He had called it Blackie. It caught mice around the back of the house, and sometimes, to his disgust, birds. Once he had taken a bird away from it and released it. The cat had gone frantically searching for it all over the flat. But the bird had flown away on its second life.

Shortly after his wife died Mrs Floss, who stayed next door, rang the doorbell.

"About the light," she said.

"The light?" said Trevor.

"Yes, every second week you put the light on. It's your turn this week. Julia knew all about it." He didn't like her calling his wife Julia with such familiarity.

"Oh," he said. "Well, I could leave it on every night if you like. Otherwise, I might forget."

"Not at all," she said. Her false teeth glittered at him, filling her mouth. She was a fat woman who swanned about in a haze of drink. She was a widow: her husband had owned an hotel.

"Oh no, that wouldn't do at all," she said.

"All right then, I'll put my light on for my own week," he said. "Is there anything else?"

"The stair," she said.

"What about the stair?"

"It has to be washed every second week." So this was what

Julia had been spending her life doing, seeing to trivialities like the stair and the light while he was writing his poetry.

"Julia used pipeclay," said Mrs Floss. "I don't know where she got it from. But I know she used pipe clay."

"Pipe clay?" said Trevor.

"Yes, that's right."

So he made sure that the light was on every second week and that the stair was cleaned every second week. Responsibilities were descending on him.

One night he heard a voice in the corridor. He couldn't think at first where it was coming from. It was Mrs Floss speaking through the letter box, reminding him that he should turn his light off as it wasn't his week. Before she could get back to her own flat he switched his light off, thus plunging her into the dark. The silly old git. If that was all that was worrying her, let her crawl through the black night.

The first letter he wrote after Julia's death was to Dr Barnardo's telling them that he would no longer be able to keep up charitable payments.

The second letter he wrote was to a company which had been sending a book a month to Julia. They had maintained for some time that she was behind with her payments which wasn't true. Any letter that was sent to them seemed to cross another one: it was like trying to send notes to a monster in the centre of a maze. Trevor wrote an angry letter.

"Dear Sirs, You advertise the works of Dickens and Trollope and other famous writers. You call them the finest spirits of their age and say we should all read the classics, because we are such helpless uneducated oafs in comparison with you. I don't understand why, if you are so civilized, you are still sending demand notes to my wife who is now dead. You can take your Dickens and your Trollope and stuff them. Yours sincerely, Trevor Porter."

He gained great satisfaction from this letter, and hoped it would arrive at the Managing Director's desk. He never heard from them again.

Boycott had made one run in half an hour. There was a spurt of ironical applause. The cat blinked and stared coolly at him.

He composed a letter to the local paper.

"I should like a woman who can pipe-clay a stair and speak a little Greek."

He changed it.

"Lady who can pipe-clay a stair and speak good English required."

He changed it again.

"Lady required for modest writer of moderate means and who likes listening to Bach. Must be able to pipe-clay a stair."

He thought of poems in which the word 'clay' would occur, he thought of Joyce's short story with that title.

The clayey faces of the shadowy Greeks.

He thought of the pipes of Pan made of clay.

"Lady of certain years required to pipe-clay stairs. Should be literate, numerate, moderate." This woman would bend down and clean the stair, decorate it. She would play on her clay pipe. Maybe, however, there was no pipe clay any more. You never knew. Maybe whoever had made pipe clay had ceased to make it. He imagined him as a small man with a beard who also played the violin in a back room in a tenement. These pipes of clay were sent all over the world. This man who had been made redundant had started his enterprise fearlessly and now he was making millions of pounds. Chinese, Indians, bought his product. His pipes told of mortality, of the earth. Pipe clay. What a wonderful combination.

One day he had a phone call from a woman he had never heard of and who, for some reason, he decided, on the basis of the voice alone, was fat and wore a string of pearls. She said that she had taken his name from a poetry directory. She was trying to save an oak tree whose branches and leaves had spread out across a road in Edinburgh and was a danger to the traffic. The tree had been planted in the eighteenth century by a Professor of Theology whose wife had committed suicide. It was a mark of respect to his wife whom he hadn't loved enough while she was alive but loved just like Thomas Hardy, after she was dead. The woman wanted to gather together a number of signatures of poets etc. in order to save the tree. She also wanted to form a committee.

"I would be no good on a committee," said Trevor.

"You never know till you try," said the woman briskly. "It would be a great help. You see, there are some little men who are complaining that the tree is an obstruction to buses."

"Oh," said Trevor.

"Yes. People with moustaches, I shouldn't wonder. I have written to them but to no avail. I suggested that they should reroute their buses; this is the oldest oak tree left in Edinburgh."

"An oak tree," thought Trevor. Ships were made of oak trees in the past. Old England was built on the oak. It cast its marvellous solid shadows. It reminded him of Newark, of Robin Hood. In the middle of the wood . . . Dante. A poem swam into his head. It was to do with Dante and an oak tree. Dante's three-lined verses were shadows cast by the oak tree.

"I'll think about it," he said. The woman seemed disappointed. She kept on at him, she said people were needed urgently. He repeated that he would think about it and put down the phone. That had been the story of his life, thinking about things, but never doing them, leaving them to his wife.

For instance, when they had come to this flat first, the roof had let in water. The tenants had told the owner it wasn't their fault. It was only a short time before that they had paid for roof repairs. Trevor didn't want to be bothered. He would have paid so that the owner would go away. If he ever thought about a problem of this nature it grew so complicated that it went to the heart of the world, the fall from Eden, and so on. It became a deep philosophical question deriving from Plato. It was a rabbinical enigma. Julia, however, was more direct. She went round the other tenants, looking for signatures. She asked Trevor to glance over the letter which she had typed impeccably and addressed to the owner. She said that none of the people in the flat would pay a penny. Not long before, they had paid £300 for repairs to the roof. Trevor was frightened that they would be evicted.

However, the owner had surrendered. Trevor felt that Julia despised him for his neutrality, but she didn't say anything. Everyone else in the flats knew that she had got them off and for a while she was very popular. Of course Mrs Miller would never have paid anyway: she would have refused on principle.

He didn't know whether he should have anything to do with the oak tree. Probably not. He had other things to do with his time. Like finding out about his life which had passed in a dream. He had never believed that Julia would die before him. Now that he was alone he felt suspended in mid-air.

One day when Julia was away for a week in Devon he locked himself out by mistake. He didn't know what to do. Then he remembered that Mrs Brown, who at that time lived above him, had a ladder and he had gone to ask for it. She had ushered him into a crowded room and said, "You will have a wee sherry?" He had sipped his sherry, looking about him all the time. The room was like a museum frozen in time. There was a radio, ornaments (mostly copper), magazines, newspapers, a stool, sideboards, mirrors, fire-irons, a pouffe. In the middle of all this Mrs Brown had offered him a sherry.

And of course the ladder.

"When you are finished, put the ladder back in the shed and throw the key through my letter box. I am going out."

Trevor steadied the ladder against the side of the house and dived in through the window, landing on the sofa. Then he opened the door and replaced the ladder in the shed. When he told Mrs Floss about the incident she roared with maniac laughter, thinking it hilariously funny. Not at all funny, thought Trevor. Julia would never have forgotten her key. He saw himself plunging on to the sofa from the blue sky like Icarus with wounded wings. Another time he left a steak in a pan and when he went to look at it, it had dwindled to a black mass the size of a piece of coal.

Living in a flat was difficult but he liked it. He liked the sense of movement around him. It was better than living in a detached or semi-detached house, especially after Julia died. He had been frightened the first night as if she would appear to him in the darkness, as if she would scrabble darkly in her room, but he had got over this fear.

There was a shop-keeper with an eye patch whom he called Nelson, and from whom he bought turnips and cabbage and carrots. Nelson said that he was sorry to hear about his wife. She was a nice woman, always cheery. It suddenly occurred to Trevor that he didn't know what his wife had been doing while he was in school. She had known people like this. She had spoken to them every day. She had friends of her own whom he didn't know about. Why had he never thought of that before?

Nelson had said to him, "Apples are a penny cheaper today."

"As much as that?" said Trevor.

Then he had left. The tenement, tall with grey stone, was his home and would now be for the rest of his days. He would have to look after the bins, the stair, the light. He would have to remember to change the curtains, hoover the rooms, dust them; that would be his work in the future.

The cat sitting like a statue stared at him. He had found it one morning at the bins, shivering wet, and had taken it in. It would sit on his shoulder and nuzzle his face. Sometimes if it didn't want petting it would strike out at him with its thorny claws.

He had got into a routine. He would wake at eight o'clock and have cornflakes and a piece of toast. After that he would switch on the radio. The unions were on strike again; there had been another train smash. Then he would cook his dinner and read in the afternoon. After tea he would watch television. He knew that sooner or later he would grow tired of the routine but for the moment he was simply trying to survive. Routine was sanity. Sometimes he would wake up in the morning, thinking that Julia was lying by his side. The disappointment he felt when he realized that she wasn't was unsettling, frightening.

44

He had a friend still teaching who would come and see him. This friend was called Richardson. He was tall, vague, unpromoted. The two of them would play chess and Richardson would fall asleep over the board and snore. After about an hour he would shake his head like a horse and apologize. By this time Trevor had forgotten why he had made his last move. Richardson wouldn't leave till three in the morning. Short of putting on his pyjamas Trevor didn't know how he should hint that it was time for him to go. He would sometimes feel that he ought to hit him with a poker.

Richardson would say, "They are thinking of making the school into a community centre. Older people would attend classes. But what are you going to do? Are you going to tell them to walk single file in the corridors?" Questions like this on the margin of things bothered him. He had applied for many promoted posts but had failed to get them. He was always complaining he had no money. "Do you see what the police are getting?" He lost and mislaid things, was a vague wandering presence. And yet Trevor had never beaten him at chess.

"You play chess like draughts," Richardson would say to him. It was true. He had never made any strategic conquests. His wars were always fought piece-meal. Actually he preferred to do chess problems than play against live opponents. Yet he didn't like Richardson saying this, for he prided himself on his intelligence.

"The high heid yins were at the school today," Richardson would say. "The litter was cleaned up. It's all a con game."

A woman called Mrs Blaney answered the advertisement for stair-woman. She was neatly dressed and wore gloves.

"I don't mind if I have a cup of tea," she said, looking round her at the roomy kitchen. "I have to go and see a friend of mine later," she said, glancing at her slim watch. The class of stair-woman had gone up, thought Trevor. This isn't what it used to be like.

"What time do you wish me to come," said Mrs Blaney in a

businesslike manner. She might have been a secretary waiting with pencil poised.

"Oh, any day would suit me," said Trevor.

"Tuesday then," said Mrs Blaney.

"Tuesday would do fine," said Trevor. "And what about pipe clay?"

"Pipe clay?"

"Yes, I believe my wife used pipe clay on the stair. So Mrs Floss says."

"Who's Mrs Floss?" (Suspicious, defensive.)

"She stays next door. She's been here for only a short time."

"I doubt if pipe clay will be available now," said Mrs Blaney decisively.

"Oh, you mean whoever made it has stopped?"

"Possibly. An hour, I think, should be sufficient. I have other places to attend to as well." She sounded like a nurse. Stairs were like decaying patients.

"I imagine," said Trevor.

"Tuesday then for an hour," said Mrs Blaney, making a note in her diary. Trevor didn't wish to introduce the sordid subject of money and she possibly assumed that he knew the going rates.

"I usually like my cup of tea afterwards," said Mrs Blaney. "My clients know that. I read the newspaper from cover to cover. That is how I noticed your advertisement."

"I hoped it might be seen," said Trevor.

"Things are not what they used to be," said Mrs Blaney, as if excusing herself for taking such a menial job, and at the same time showing Trevor that she wasn't just any old staircleaner.

"I have a son in university. They are so selfish nowadays, the young. Do you find that? Have you any children?"

"One son."

"I see. Much more selfish than we were. I was brought up in the country and when I was young I used to cut bracken all day for a shilling. I used to give my wages to my mother. The young don't pay for their keep nowadays, and if you ask them they say they didn't want to be brought into the world anyway. And they talk of nuclear war. As if that had anything to do with it."

"I agree with you," said Trevor.

"You ask them for money or anything of theirs and they won't give it to you, but all your possessions are theirs if they want them. Have you noticed that? I have never seen such selfishness. Do you know what my son was doing when he was home last weekend? Looking for the gold watch my husband left. He kept searching in all the drawers. I said to him, 'That watch isn't yours.' 'Why not,' he said. 'That watch is a mason's watch.' I told him. 'And the ring is the same. It's got G written on it. You're not a mason, are you?' But he kept looking for it just the same."

Trevor had made the mistake of giving her a mug with her tea. She kept staring at it and sometimes touching the rim with the tip of her finger as if it was infected. He made a note that next time he would give her the special cups with the blue and white stripes.

"And they're so unmannerly. A friend of mine has a sister who is very hoity toity and she came to visit them. Her son came in drunk and tried to dance with her. She was so ashamed, so embarrassed. He also tried to borrow money from her.

"Oh, there is one thing," she said. "You could give me my fare for the bus as well as the money for the stair, which I think should be three pounds. I hope you consider that reasonable."

"I'm sure," said Trevor, who didn't know much about the economics of stair-washing.

Mrs Blaney got to her feet, slipping on her gloves again. "I shall start next week since you tell me this is not your week for the stair. I shall be here at three o'clock prompt in the afternoon. My son will be back in university. His lecturers of course are as bad as the students. One of them said as he fell over a paper basket in the classroom, 'You want me to kick the bucket, I suppose.' He comes in late and I believe he's a Communist. Sometimes he doesn't appear at all. They are as selfish as the students. And then I've to make his bed whenever he comes home. He always leaves his room in a mess and the bathroom light on during the night. You can't tell them anything, they know it all. Recently I heard of a girl of twelve who wanted to bring ten friends home for a birthday party. And their boy friends as well, she said. 'No way,' said her mother. 'In that case, I'll book an hotel room,' she said. At twelve years old! Well, thank you for the tea." And she made her way to the door which Trevor opened for her as if she were royalty.

Trevor's son was called Robin. He was married to a primary school teacher and they now lived in Cambridge with a little daughter whom they were bringing up to be exactly like themselves.

One day she said to Trevor, "You owe me ten pence." It had all arisen from a complicated transaction involving ice cream. But it struck him that at a very early age she was showing the ugly face of capitalism.

His son had been born when he was in the war fighting for Britain. His mother idolized him. His grandfather, who had been a miner, fought with him in mock sport.

When he was ten he asked his father, "Why are we always moving about?"

Trevor had not answered him. The continual shifting had made Robin nervous and the consequence was that he became remote and enclosed. He was now a computer operator. He had always been good at maths but not at English. In fact he constantly failed his English exams till the final year when he had somehow passed his Highers.

His mother would say to him, "Your father will help you with your poetry", but he refused help. He hated poetry. People were always reading into poetry what wasn't there, or only tenuously.

When he was fourteen he started work in the Co-op in the evenings. He would never give Trevor any money: he turned out to be very mean. Trevor wondered if that was because he felt insecure and felt sorry for him, but later the meanness made him angry. He was always asking what he would get for his birthday, but never gave Trevor a present for his.

He had been laughed at, by the other children, when his father had been teaching in the same school. They bullied him. When he complained, his father told him that he would have to learn to defend himself, but his mother, from a sense of outraged justice, said that she would go and see the headmaster. Trevor knew that his own reason for saying what he said was that he was a coward and afraid to interfere. However, he had prevented Julia from visiting the headmaster. Ever since then Robin despised him as he had expected protection and received none. Trevor felt that Julia despised him as well, as she watched her son being miserable and ignoring his lessons.

That meanness, that egocentricity, where had it come from? Had it come from pain? Did he not have enough energy to think of other people?

Eventually Trevor didn't like his son at all. He thought of him as some kind of monster, mathematical, silent, spoiling his daughter who would become a monster as well. There were one or two occasions when Julia had pointed out a good review of Trevor's poems in a newspaper but Robin wouldn't read them. In fact he made a point of ignoring them.

After his wife died, Trevor had a nightmare. He was in Newark, and firing arrows through a wood, he hit Julia and Robin whose faces were like giant dartboards. Suddenly Robin had the sheriff's face and his wife had a greenish tinge on hers as she ran away from him bleeding among the leaves like a deer. He had wakened up in a sweat.

One day Robin came to visit him. They sat together in the big kitchen with the jars arranged and labelled on the shelves, just as Julia had left them.

"How are you," said Robin. He was dressed in a new suit and looked like an executive, his black shining hair neatly brushed.

"I'm fine," said Trevor gruffly. "How are you all?"

"Fine. Sheila sends her love. Are you managing on your own?"

"I'm managing."

"Still writing?" said Robin contemptuously.

"Not much."

"I see. I thought when you were once on your own you would write a great deal."

"Well, I don't. Do you yourself computerize much?"

"I'm here for a meeting. I'll be going back tonight. I thought I'd call in and see how you were."

"Well, I'm fine. Look around you. Can't you see that everything is neat and tidy? I can look after the flat."

"You should maybe sell it. It's very large. You should perhaps move into a smaller flat."

"Why?"

"I thought it would be more manageable and cheaper."

"No, I shall stay here," said Trevor firmly.

"I see."

Was he wondering why he had ceased to move only after his mother died? Sometimes Trevor wondered whether he himself had caused his wife's cancer. Perhaps if you moved too much during your life you got cancer. It was the disease of the wandering deviant cells. Maybe his own poetry had saved him from the cancer. It was true he hadn't written much recently. Loneliness wasn't conducive to great art. Why had Robin come to torment him? Had he come to gloat over him in his solitude? Had he hoped to see the flat in a mess as his own room had once been, with socks lying over chairs, sweaty jerseys and ties lying on the bed, football boots lying aslant on the floor?

"I have a woman who comes to do the stair," said Trevor mischievously. "She has a son at university doing Business Studies. She is well spoken. I wouldn't be surprised if she read Beckett."

"I see," said Robin again. He was always saying 'I see'. Why did he look like a comic executive? Why was he so humourless, why did he think so slowly, calculate so much? He was perhaps working out that his father would leave him the flat which would fetch a good price on the market. Unless he married the stair-woman. Was that why he had come? He was always thinking about money, he wore a kind of silver armour. Maybe he thinks the stair-woman and myself will live together forever, with our pipe clay, thought Trevor. He smiled and Robin didn't know what he was smiling at, and he felt uneasy. He was an old selfish bastard. He had killed his mother, that was for sure. He didn't know that he and his mother had kept up a close correspondence and phoned each other three times a week. He, Robin, gave her some money but nothing to his old man with his stupid poetry, as if it mattered a damn.

Trevor was glad to see the back of his son. He didn't like being patronized. He and Robin had nothing in common. Robin calculated every move, saw his daughter's teachers, made sure that she contributed money to the blacks: some of her pocket money went to a girl in Nigeria. But there was nothing spontaneous about all that. It was in fact a sort of affectation. He is a monster, thought Trevor, but didn't blame himself. If you blamed yourself for everything you would go mad.

When he went to collect his pension he stared with nostalgia at the bums of the young girls in jeans. They looked like peaches, apples. Oh Lord, he thought, I'm growing old, and this was emphasized to him when, dropping his pension book one day in the post office, one of the young girls bent down and retrieved it for him. "There you are, sir," she said.

Never again would he approach that remembered country, never again.

The woman phoned about the oak tree, but he put her off again. However, he went for a walk one day and sat under an oak tree in the small town where he lived. He loved the cool shade of its branches. Beside him on the green seat with bubbles of rain still on it was a military-looking man with a bristling moustache. The man talked to him about India, a subject apparently dear to his heart. He was simplistic, anachronistic. Trevor could hardly believe that such a person could exist. In his crushed hat he sat meekly listening. Yes, the British had ruled India well, hadn't they? The leaves of the oak stirred in the breeze. The tree was ancient too, presumably like the one in Edinburgh. But Trevor saw too many sides of a question. He was not a Fortinbras like this empire builder beside him, he was a Hamlet. After all, shouldn't buses have their right of way as well?

"Should never have come home," said the military man. "Biggest mistake of my life." He talked of how he had travelled one day by train to Glasgow. It had been two hours late. He ran to a phone to tell his hosts of his mishap but the phones were all broken, vandalized. What kind of country was this, falling about our ears? Just like an old tenement, thought Trevor, and recalled Cameron, that fat slob who beat up his wife at weekends. Others played golf, he beat up his wife. It was his recreation. Julia had told him to go to the police, but the police wouldn't do anything about it. Domestic problem, they had said. This great country of ours sheltered its brutes under the shade of its oak tree. He blamed Cameron for Julia's death. She never got any peace. And he hated Cameron, hated him with a deadly hatred, more than he hated Hitler. It was Cameron who wouldn't let Julia sleep. Yes, he agreed with the military man. Violence everywhere. Loss of standards. and so the two of them sat under the oak tree, watching the pure white swans on the lake.

He had been tormented by a boy called Sherman in his classes. This Sherman would come in to school early and write his nickname on the blackboard. Then he would make animal noises at the back of the room and Trevor would never be able to pin him down. Sherman would say, "Please sir, I can't think of anything to write in my composition." And Trevor would say, "But you must be able to think of something." "I can't think of anything at all," Sherman would say, smiling. And maybe Trevor would try and belt him and Sherman would pull his hand away. So Trevor would take him to the headmaster and Sherman, who was an actor, would tremble as if he were afraid of Trevor and the headmaster would say to himself, "Ah, there is more to this than meets the eye." And he would regard Sherman, who wasn't at all loutish or terrifying, as a victim who patiently endured Trevor's sarcasm and beatings. And he would say to him, "Now you promise me that you will be a good boy", and of course Sherman would say he would, not omitting the 'sir'. Trevor thought that Sherman was evil, that he had never encountered unprincipled evil till he had met him. His cunning and his intelligence were extraordinary, his methods of putting Trevor in the wrong legion. Sometimes after he had pulled his hand away he would say that Trevor had broken his watch. He had an inexhaustible supply of broken watches. Trevor imagined a factory which produced broken watches, something like British Leyland. Sherman too had the knack of enticing him away from the theme of the lesson down byways of his own. Trevor hated him and hated also his mother and father whom he had encountered. Sherman was one of the reasons why he had left Newark. Sherman was the Robin Hood who ran about the green wood tormenting him, firing arrows at him, smiling at him, the outlaw hero. And he himself was the clumsy sheriff, always outwitted. In the free wood.

"Yes," he said to the military looking man. "I agree with you totally." He pulled down his hat and walked away.

Sometimes he met Mrs Miller on the stair, but she never talked to him. At first there had been Mrs Brown and then there were the Camerons. He often ran into Cooper when he was putting stuff in the bin, but Cooper always seemed to be in a hurry. His work in the summer was looking after lavatories.

It was Mrs Floss who told him about the old man, Mr Butcher, of whose existence Trevor had been entirely unaware. But apparently Julia used to visit him and help him as best she could.

"I don't know where he stays but it's somewhere on the street," said Mrs Floss, who had come back from a world cruise paid for with her dead husband's money. "She used to tell me about him. We had a coffee together now and again. Your wife was a wise, kind woman. I used to tell her about Stewart when he was on drugs and she would give me good advice. She was never too busy to pass you by." Mrs Floss thought that about Trevor, however. She felt that he was snooty, superior, but then on the other hand, it might just be that he was shy. Still, his wife was worth ten of him any day. She was human, warm, she even tried to help Mrs Miller, that selfish old bag upstairs. But Trevor never helped anyone. He would pass her on the stair muttering under his breath as if he were thinking furiously. And yet he had only been a teacher. He hadn't seen as much of the world as she had and yet he had this absurd sense of superiority. She could tell him a thing or two. And he hardly ever remembered about the light, no matter how often she reminded him. And why didn't that stair-woman use pipe clay: Julia used to make beautiful patterns on the stair: she was very artistic. Always patient too, and long suffering. She didn't know where Mr Butcher stayed. Trevor could ask the postman.

One day when Julia and Trevor were in Ilfracombe in Devon they made a mistake and instead of turning up a road which would take them back to the town, they turned up another one instead. They came to a farmhouse which had bright rough tables in front of it, and had in fact been converted into a restaurant. They sipped their iced drinks and then Trevor picked up from the table a brochure which told them the history of the farmhouse. It was called the Haunted House. Many years before, when the coast had been notorious for wreckers, a man used to light fires to bring ships on to the rocks. Then he would plunder them for their cargo. His daughter had left and gone to America to make her fortune. One night he saw a ship and set his illusory lights. The ship had gone on the rocks. He searched the cabins for jewellery and other plunder and found in one of them a woman who was dead and in fact his daughter. He took her body home with him and walled it up in his farm-house.

Many years later the wife of the farmer who then owned the

house said she was going to market. Her husband sat on a bench outside in the sun reading his paper. After a while his attention wandered and he idly studied the house and saw the outline of a window where as far as he knew there was no room. Calculating that there had been a room there in the past, he got hold of some of his workmen and they broke down the wall. And there behind the wall was a room and on an ancient bed the skeleton of a woman. There was also some jewellery. It was some of the money from selling it that had been used to build the restaurant. The owner told the two of them that an American woman, who said that she had spiritual powers sensitive to auras, had been in the room—now open to visitors—and she had seen a woman in white, with seaweed in her hair, walking about; there was jewellery around her neck. Her face was green.

As they walked away from the Haunted House in the bright sunlight, Julia ahead, Trevor imagined that he could see her very bones, so transparent she was in her light dress. She looked vulnerable, thin. He had shivered then in that bright sunshine, haunted by the past, its greed and selfishness.

The postman was able to tell him where Mr Butcher lived.

"Very tragic about Mrs Porter," said Mr Butcher. "She used to come here of a Thursday afternoon and sometimes of a Tuesday afternoon as well."

He sat down opposite Trevor, holding a stick in his hands. "She used to make a cup of tea and bring me my messages."

His keen blue eyes stared unwinkingly at Trevor. There were soup stains on his jacket.

"She was younger than us of course. I always felt better for talking to her."

What did they talk about?

"Oh, I used to be a seaman. We talked about ports, Hong Kong, Auckland, places like that. I been all over the world. I think she wanted to move."

"What are you saying, you old bastard," said Trevor under his breath. "She often wished she had a proper house and a garden.

She talked about Devon. She talked about her son and her grand-daughter. She missed seeing her grand-daughter."

And all that time she never told me, thought Trevor. She wanted a part of her life which she could have for her own. He felt angry that she should have confided in this smelly old man.

"A good woman," the latter was saying. "She never complained. My legs is bad, you see. I have trouble climbing the stair. Would you like a cup of tea?"

Two old men together.

No, I don't want any of your tea. Trevor felt obscurely jealous of the old man, of the conversations that he had never heard. It was as if there had been a side to his wife that he had never known about, and it bothered him.

"She would have made a good nurse," Butcher was saying. "She told me once she'd wanted to be a nurse, but her parents were against it. So she became a secretary instead. That was how you met, wasn't it, at school?"

"Yes," said Trevor between his teeth.

In a short while you're going to say, How old do you think I am? And I'll say you're sixty-five though you're nearer eighty. The old man's teeth lay in a cup on the window sill like sharks' teeth under water.

"She said you was very busy. 'Always busy,' she said. 'A Head of a Department is always busy,' she said."

The tears came into Trevor's eyes. So that had worried her and yet she had told him it hadn't. When they were romancing in their youth she had told him that they could live happily in a cottage together. Yet all this time she had been worried about a house and a garden and his position. A bee buzzed in the old man's room, trying to get out. There were ships in bottles on the sideboard. So much he had seen of the world that Trevor hadn't. All he had seen were the grey ships on wintry nights while below them like mice under floorboards the U-boats patrolled restlessly.

He was furious with the old man. God damn him! What was that about being Head of a Department? His wife had gone to him for talk like a beggar, she had felt the time long; it was she perhaps who needed therapy.

The old man limped over to the window and opened it. The bee still battered itself against the glass. Stupid insect, blind, blundering, honeyed.

"I was shattered when I heard of her death. Of course she told me she had cancer. But she wasn't frightened. She had worked out how long she had. She was a brave lady. Nothing but cancer wherever you look. I've no reason to complain. I've only got arthritis."

No reason to complain. The sentimental sweetness of it. We are summoned into this world, catapulted on our mission as if with a parachute: youth deceives us, age makes us cynics: the grandeur departs and we lie in harbour becalmed.

There was a verse of poetry above the old man's sideboard.

> Build a little fence of trust
>   around today.
> Fill the space with loving work
>   and therein stay.
> Look not through the sheltering bars
>   upon tomorrow.
> God will help thee bear what comes
>   of joy or sorrow.

What immortal poetry, what resonance, what Miltonic sonority! And yet it had probably helped the old man more than Shakespeare would have done.

"My own wife died two years ago. She didn't know me at the end. She would sit opposite me and say, 'Who is that man? Who are you? Go away, I don't want to see you. I want my Ralph back' (that's me). And she would say, 'What house is this? I want to go back to my own house'. She would sometimes hear the cry of a baby in the bedroom during the night. 'Why don't you look after the baby', she would say. Most of the time I was abroad, you see. I was an engineer. She thought I was a stranger who had got into the house. She would say funny things like, 'What am I to do with my face?' 'What do you want to do with your face', I'd say, and she would say, 'I want to put it out'. You would give her an ashtray for her cigarette and she would still put the ash on the floor. One time she said, 'Who do I have to ask permission from to stop smoking?' 'No one', I'd say, but she wouldn't believe me. She would make you really laugh. Still, she liked the ships in the bottles."

Trevor got to his feet, saying, "I just came along to see you."

"Welcome any time," said the old man. "Very good of you." Two old men together, thought Trevor again.

Butcher was lighting his pipe as he left. Trevor walked down stairs which weren't pipecleaned. He heard the roar of a TV from one of the flats. A woman was shouting, "Can't you give me a moment's peace?" Clothes hung on a rope on the back green, flat and geometrical.

"Would you believe it?" said Mrs Blaney, balancing the cup of tea on her knee. "I asked him for the loan of fifty pence to pay the papers the other day and he wouldn't give it to me. Refused point blank. Said he was going to a dance. Sometimes he comes in at seven o'clock in the morning. I have to keep awake all night. He'll throw me a jacket and say 'Sew a button on for me', no please or anything else, as if I was a servant. Do this, do that, that's their style. They're like seagulls, never satisfied. A little touch of sugar, please."

Trevor pushed the sugar bowl across. "It's not good for me of course. I've tried to slim but I always surrender in the end. Always. I saw a diet in the *Express* the other day, melons and cucumbers mostly. They tell you to take milk, then they tell you not to take it. They tell you whisky is good for you. Mind you, it said in the paper the other day that a tot *is* good for you. I don't suppose you're in for the million pounds? They want to sell more papers, that's what it is. I don't know what I would do if I got a million pounds. So many people get a divorce when they become rich, don't you think? Look at Elizabeth Taylor and Richard Burton."

Trevor considered them. He hated Elizabeth Taylor. He thought she was a totally selfish hardbitten survivor. He had a photograph of her on the wall opposite the toilet seat. She was smiling at her fifth husband and saying "This time it's for keeps." She was as sweet as a young girl. How did they do it, these people? How did they walk through crashing marriages? He had never wanted anyone other than Julia. He had loved her and she had loved him.

"I have a card with my number on it for the million pounds," said Mrs Blaney. "But the fact is, I've never won anything in a raffle. The number of raffle tickets I've bought you would never believe. I'm not a lucky person. Well, thank you for the tea. I'll be here again week after next. There's no pipe clay available, I told you that. I don't know where your wife got it from, I tried everywhere. No pipe clay, they told me, they don't make it now. It's like these coloured clips for spectacles, different colours. You stick them on the frames. Well, you can't get them any more. I've asked a lot of opticians. We've discontinued that line, they say. And they were beautiful and so handy. Still."

She pulled on her gloves. "That woman next door, what's her name?"

"Mrs Floss," said Trevor.

"Does she often wander about in her nightgown?"

"Not always. A lot of the time. She goes on world tours."

"Oh, oh, well, some people have all the luck. Ta ta, then, see you week after next."

Trevor picked the letter from the floor and glanced through it rapidly. "Pleased to ask you to talk to our group . . . small number of people interested in poetry . . . of course not as good as you and others like you. Would August the 7th be suitable? Will be done through. . . . Meet you at station if you wish. . . . Look forward to seeing you. . . . Such a treat for our people . . . real live author. . . . One of our members had a poem in the

People's Journal, another a story in Nickety Nackety. . . . BBC programme. . . . Yours Very Sincerely, Marjorie Gillespie. PS Would be glad if you would consent to judge our entries for the FLORA NICOLSON SHORT STORY CUP."

Trevor laughed quietly to himself. Sometimes he blew into small towns for poetry readings like a hit man with his briefcase. So many people he had met at draughty stations. So many had stood up and said, "Needs no introduction. One of Scotland's . . ." Sometimes there might be thirty people, sometimes three. Once a member of the audience had shouted "Are you a committed poet?" One of his poems which used fishing as a linguistic metaphor had led to a discussion with an old trawler man about cod . . . his voice echoed across empty seats. Was he the god they had come to see, the one touched by fire from heaven? Not at all. Once someone had asked him, "Do you feel yourself a poet when you get up in the morning?" "No," Trevor had replied honestly.

Once he had been introduced as Hector Macmaster, a lyricist of note. At the end of the proceedings he shoved his cheque in his wallet and ran away, with his ancient briefcase.

After each poetry reading he washed his face. How unclean he felt. Unclean, unclean. Should he have a bell like a leper?

He wrote: "Pleased to visit your group. Thank you for asking me. Yes, the time stated will be suitable. Would be glad if you would meet me at the station bookstall at half past six. Will judge your short stories. Always wish to encourage creativity. Yours sincerely, Trevor Porter."

Dynamo of the Muses, Road Traveller, Hit Man of the Poetry Society. Who is the best poet on your avenue?

Boycott had made twenty runs. Trevor couldn't understand why he liked watching cricket so much, even though he had never played it. He liked perhaps the leisurely desultory eternal hum of it, the commentators with their plummy voices, the old fashioned terminology, the ritual, the silences . . . the shadows cast on the ground by the white uniforms. Good old Boycott. Remain yourself at all costs. Don't let anyone hurry you.

One day Julia's sister, Patricia, and her husband, James, drove all the way from Devon in James' car. James wasn't in the habit of speaking much, though he could drive a tractor, repair it, run a farm, build a house, sing when requested to at concerts, cook and do innumerable other things. His wife, Patricia, said, "I only came to collect the brooch my mother passed on to Julia, I hope you don't mind."

"Not at all," said Trevor.

James stared down at the floor with its blue linoleum. When Trevor and Julia had visited them in Devon they would be wakened by a cock crowing. He had been taught how to drive a tractor, but wasn't really interested in the farm. On the other hand he could do any electrical repairs required.

"So sad," said Patricia. "James drove me up. It's a holiday for me but James here doesn't like taking holidays. He hasn't had a holiday for fifteen years, have you, James?" James stared down at the floor, his face red and ripe like a fruit. "I wouldn't really want anything," said Patricia, "but the brooch has a sentimental value." Trevor took her into Julia's room. There were brushes, pots of powder, lipstick, bath salts, soaps, lying on the dressing table.

"So sad," Patricia repeated. "Julia wanted a house. Did you know that? She hated living in a flat. Why didn't you take a school in Devon? She wanted to return there. There was a young boy she nearly married. He had a motor cycle, but mother never liked him. She thought motor cycles were dangerous."

Together we walked along the cliffs, thought Trevor, as in Hardy's poems. He too had never known how much he had loved his wife until he lost her, selfish, bald, old man. Yet those heartbreaking poems! By the cliffs. There was a flash of Julia turning her face towards him against the blinding yellow of the mustard seed.

". . . naturally she thought of you as well. We corresponded regularly. She was the only one of my sisters I wrote to. Ah, well."

James hadn't spoken at all. Perhaps he felt ashamed of his wife with her bright seeking eyes.

"Take anything you like," said Trevor. "I'm sure she would like you to take anything."

"Are you sure? Well, then, this other brooch . . . I like it very much. So unusual. It will be a memory of her."

"Certainly."

"You won't be moving to a smaller flat?"

"No."

"Wasn't there a couple here who were making a lot of noise? It got on Julia's nerves, I remember her telling me."

"Yes."

"Are they still as bad?"

"Yes. Unfortunately."

"She did so much travelling, poor dear. She hated packing, unpacking. Didn't she, James?"

James muttered some incomprehensible words. His red hands lay on his knees. The cleverest of the lot of us, thought Trevor, he doesn't speak at all. Everything comes so easily to him and yet his wife leads him by the hand. Odd. What does he really think about? Is he a philosopher in his deepest being?

"Of course I don't drive myself," said Patricia brightly. "We came through London. I don't know how James does it. First time we came through London in the car and he had no difficulty. No, thanks, we won't wait for a cup of tea really. You see so many foreign cars driving in the middle of the road. Isn't that right, James? They have no idea. Of course we don't leave Devon much."

Take the jewellery and go, thought Trevor viciously.

"There weren't many at the funeral," said Patricia. "I thought there might have been more."

"I shall be cremated myself," said Trevor irrelevantly.

"Oh? She should have been sent to Devon among her own people. That's what I was saying to James."

They left, James shaking Trevor's hand in an embarrassed manner. Trevor slammed the door, thought of the bare dressing table and wept.

He listened to the din above his head. The Camerons fighting again. "Bugger you," he shouted in fury and banged at the ceiling with his broom. There was silence for a while, then the noise restarted as if Cameron were moving wardrobes, sideboards, gravestones, from corner to corner. What on earth was he doing? Could a man be as evil as to do that, create noise for the sake of doing so? Trevor wept tears of shame and anger. He should have confronted that lout long ago, but he had never had the courage. "You killed my wife," he shouted. There was another silence and then the TV was turned on full blast. Cameron was undoubtedly a psychopath.

One afternoon, quite by chance, he found what his wife had been looking for when she had painfully left her bed. It was a diary, hidden between two sheets in a drawer. It had a pink cover. Trevor withdrew it carefully: he wouldn't have found it unless he had been looking for sheets to change the bed.

The diary began at the time when he was in the Navy and told of the birth of Robin, of his schooling, of his beginning work. (Trevor asks him to give money to me but he refuses!) Later, however, he read that Robin had been sending money to his mother secretly. (But nothing for the old bugger, so he calls him. I wish he wouldn't speak like that. It's just that Trevor is occupied with his poetry. If there is no mail he's in a bad temper for the rest of the day. He talks about how others worse than him have a better literary reputation. He says he should never have left Scotland, that was his mistake.)

She confided her longings to her diary. She wanted a house. She hated the continual shifting. She wrote, "I don't want to tell him I've got cancer. It'll worry him: it doesn't worry me as much as I thought it would." (But, thought Trevor, if she had really been happy, would it not have worried her?)

63

"The fact is, he can't face reality," Julia wrote. "He wouldn't be able to face the fact of cancer any more than he could demand that repairs should be done to the roof."

She wrote, "I don't think he likes Robin because he's different from himself. He never really wanted a child, that's the tragedy of it." She underlined the words, "He must be protected." "I worry what will happen when I die and he won't be able to cope. These poetry groups, why is it always women who are in charge of them?"

"That was an odd incident at Ilfracombe," she wrote. "Unbelievable really. I thought he might have used it in a poem. But he didn't. He wants to forget about it for some reason. *I think I know.* He actually thinks I don't understand him but to me he's as clear as water, as crystal."

"I don't think he ever recovered from his experiences on the convoy. He's not really very brave. But he can endure, oh, he can certainly endure."

"I was ashamed about the flowers for the church. I should really have my own garden. I always loved gardens."

"Mrs Floss isn't too bad. Drinks too much of course but we've had lots of conversations. She's very lonely too. She told me she once fell in love with a Spaniard. And Mr Cameron. Why does he hurt his wife so much? He must know he's doing it."

"I think I should destroy this diary. I can't bring myself to do it today. Maybe tomorrow."

And that was the last entry. In the diary were details of all the places they had been to, from London to Newark to Glasgow. It detailed his continual complaints about his jobs. If it was not one thing, it was another. The entries grew shorter as Julia weakened. She had even told the doctor not to inform Trevor of what was wrong with her. But did she really love him? Would she have gone so gladly to her death if she had? He had the impression of a tired exhausted woman who wished to go to a place where there would be no more removals.

Trevor stared open eyed at the terrible naked day.

So gladly into that good night.

64

Her eyes at the end followed him everywhere as if she were wanting to ask a question.

The woman phoned about the oak tree again. He discovered that her name was Mrs Ross. He prevaricated, said he would give an answer in a few days' time. Could she leave her phone number? Time was short, she insisted. The oak tree had been there for a long time. Why could he not give an answer, he asked himself. He must change. He must change.

Travelling on the train to the poetry reading he gazed out at the fields which were orderly, neat. Suddenly he had an idea. He combined the neat fields with Dante's poetry. Dante's head like the sun appearing through the haze stared down at these geometrical fields. He took out his pen and began to write.

"These orderly fields. What would Dante say?"

The sun glared down on them, the harvesters waved out of the inferno. Who was that old woman scarfed like a tinker who was waving her handkerchief at the train? This however, unlike Dante's, was not a Catholic country. This was a sparse Protestant country. And yet Dante's verse hadn't been ornate: on the contrary, it too had been sparse.

His mind left the fields, concentrated on the train. Its carriages were like segments of worms. Dante headed through the fields like a great poet who was composed of heat, of the worm. He felt for the first time since Julia's death that a poetic idea was writhing within him. He would lay it carefully in the back of his mind as into a drawer, and let it ferment there.

Marjorie Gillespie met him at the station. She was a tall definite woman who wore tweeds.

"Would you like some dinner?" she said, skilfully negotiating the traffic in her Renault. "I booked a table for two in the Oriel Hotel."

For some reason Trevor told her that his wife had died

recently. "Oh, I am so sorry. I didn't know. Did you notice that fellow driving straight through the lights and they talk of woman drivers. Sorry, you were saying. Oh, about your wife. If I had known of course I wouldn't have intruded on you."

"Oh, that's all right. It'll be good for me." He thought for some reason that she was a teacher of Foreign Languages. She had that cool competent look. And she wore those attachments on her glasses that the stair-woman had been talking about. They were blue to match her costume. Her hair which had once been black had streaks of grey in it.

"I hope you'll like the hotel," she said. "It's quite old but it does a good dinner." They eventually reached it. It was quiet and they sat together at a table, near the window.

"Melon for me, I think," she said to the waitress.

"And the same for me," said Trevor.

"It is so awful when someone dies. Perhaps you're right. Perhaps it's better for you to be taken out of yourself." She ate her melon. "It is better than brooding, I think. I'm afraid I myself never married." She didn't look deprived. She was clearly one of those self-sufficient people who can live on their own without difficulty.

"There will be a few people here tonight. Some of course of our group are on holiday. They are shy, so they might not ask many questions. Do you mind being asked questions?"

"Not at all," said Trevor.

"Of course they don't have much knowledge of the higher reaches of literature," said Miss Gillespie, disposing of the last of her melon. "They try, you know how it is."

"Yes," said Trevor, "of course."

"I suppose you must do a lot of this?" said Miss Gillespie, choosing veal.

"I do," said Trevor, choosing fish. His hand hovered over the cabbage.

"Do you like doing it?"

"Depends on the mood I'm in."

She appeared satisfied with this. Trevor didn't want to talk too much. Sometimes he had to drag words out of the depths of his mind by conscious effort.

Miss Gillespie wiped her fingers on her red napkin. He wondered if she had ever read any of his poems.

"We had . . . and . . . here, last year," mentioning a brace of well-known poets. "They were very good. . . . told me that he hated poetry readings. He said that he always tried to be funny. That, he told me, was the great danger." Her earnest eyes interrogated Trevor. "Is that the case?"

"Yes," said Trevor.

"One of them said, I can't remember which one, that he had once been asked to pay to get into one of his own poetry readings!"

"That can happen," said Trevor.

"Imagine that!" The ways of artists were strange, romantic, exotic.

"Is there, I mean, is there much money in it? Can one live on what one makes from poetry readings?"

"I couldn't live on poetry alone," said Trevor. "But I have my pension. I taught for forty years."

Miss Gillespie was content. She had found someone who could fill a space in her programme, and Trevor didn't appear to be particularly nervous, not like the last speaker but one. Trevor liked her, she was quite like Julia, competent, but cooler, not the sort of person who would make heroic gestures or be assailed by sudden surges of compassion.

They had trifle.

"Wine?"

"No," said Trevor. She appeared to be relieved.

The poetry reading went off well. The audience consisted of 21 people who hadn't heard of him, he knew that. He stood up, after laying his crushed hat on the table and read quietly. He made some statements about literature in general. At one point he quoted Valéry. "The first line of a poem comes from God: the rest you have to work for." He told a story about a poet who

67

wanted to write a poem about flying and had learnt to pilot a one-seated plane. He told of an artist who wanted to paint the French coast and had talked at great length to the fishermen first. There were two people taking notes. One was a schoolgirl in green uniform, the other was a woman with white hair.

When the readings were over they asked him a few questions. He felt happy, satiated. For a moment he was the centre of attention, the expert. Their questions confirmed that they had never read any of his poems. One man in glasses asked him what he thought of the sonnet. Trevor said it was no longer very fashionable.

"Why is modern poetry so unintelligible," he was asked.

He went on about this for a long time. When it was all over he was driven to the station by Miss Gillespie. "One of our most successful evenings," she said judicially.

Of course it had been successful. When was anything ever unsuccessful?

"I think they learned a great deal." She shook hands with him firmly, like a man. After he had left her he found himself at a kiosk in the station. He was phoning his own house to tell Julia that he was on his way home when he remembered that she was dead. He turned away and sat for an hour in the waiting room before the train arrived.

He thought of himself as Robinson Crusoe. He had left the ship and was sometimes returning to it to retrieve mirrors, jewellery. The birds mocked him from the trees. He had ideas like, What will happen if I go blind? He considered language. The floor was like sand, brittle, numerous. There was a big Bible which his father had once used, and on which were written the names of the members of the family. Once in a dream he danced through a wood. Julia was there, Maid Marian, she was dancing towards him. They met in sunlight.

"I killed you," he told her.

"No, no, you didn't. Of course you didn't. I loved you. You were my child."

68

"You loved me more than Robin?" he asked her. But she didn't answer. They walked together, hand in hand, towards a rock which was lopsided in the water. There was a big mirror in which he saw faces, wrinkled and old.

He pointed downwards.

"Whose are these?" he asked.

"The footprints?" she said.

Footprints in the sand.

He knew he had some way to go yet. The Camerons nagged at the back of his mind.

MR COOPER WAS a retired milkman. He often stood at the door of the close, talking to people, for he was an inveterate gossip who liked company. Opposite him on the same landing were the Masons who had shifted from the flat above after the matron died. When his wife was alive Mr Cooper had a black and white television set. Now he had a coloured one which he could control by a gadget which could change channels from a distance.

Mr Cooper worked in a toilet during the summer. He had plenty of customers to talk to there: and he kept the toilet very clean. Sometimes he told his customers that he had been head of a dairy and had passed examinations. Actually, he had left school at fifteen, had served in the army during the war: he and his wife had no children. He couldn't make head or tail of Trevor Porter whom he thought slightly nuts. Mrs Floss amused him. The Camerons he didn't like. "If I was younger," he would often say, "I would beat him up. No one should ever hit a woman."

Actually the Masons didn't like him much. He was always talking to Mrs Mason, who was expecting a baby, and she told her husband that there was something odd about him. Whenever she came out of the flat to collect the coal he would say, "I'll take that in for you. You shouldn't be carrying heavy things." She was sure that he was always watching her legs when she bent down for the coal. His face was red with high blood pressure, and the sun. He often made comical remarks, but nevertheless she didn't like him. Neither did John. Many of his stories were dirty, sexual. John called him an old pervert.

"Don't make trouble," she told him. "After all, he's lost his wife."

"That's why. Because he was an old pervert. She couldn't stand it."

John worked in the freezer shop. He was always looking for a job that would bring in better money. His mother came to visit them and so did his father. Once John had thrown his father out because he was an alcoholic and insulting to his wife. "You old bugger, clear out of here or I'll floor you. Don't you realize Linda is pregnant?" But his father insisted on coming back and he did floor him. He had a taxi called and dumped him like a sack of potatoes outside his house, in the moonlight. "You should leave him," he told his mother.

"If I see Cooper sniffing around here any more, I'll clock him too," he told Linda.

"He doesn't mean any harm," said Linda.

"I'll tell you: he was always talking and joking to you when his wife was lying there ill. It wasn't right. No wonder she died. He broke her heart."

"You're exaggerating," said Linda.

"I'm not exaggerating and you know it. I can't stand people like that."

Mrs Cooper had died of heart trouble. She had been taken latterly to the hospital and had died there very quickly. A policewoman had come and told Cooper. It was eleven o'clock on a winter's night, cold and frosty.

"I couldn't believe it," he had said more than once. "I think these surgeons are no good; criminals. There was nothing wrong with her when I left her. She was talking to me quite happily when I said cheerio to her at eight o'clock." He had been really shaken by his wife's death, but he had coped better than Trevor. Perhaps his imagination was less fertile, perhaps he had a stronger sense of his own identity. He much preferred Mrs Porter: at least she would talk to you.

Mr Cooper had lived in his flat for years. He could tell the other tenants about those who had inhabited the building in the past. "Where you are," he told Linda, "there was once a boy and his mother. He wasn't quite right in the head. I suppose he must be thirty now. No, I'm a liar, he must be older than that, perhaps thirty-six. I don't know what he is doing now. At one time he used to work on the bookstall, but he wouldn't speak to anyone. So he left there. The two of them left the town. I don't know where they are now. There was also a shoemaker here, a fat fellow called Robertson. He used to make shoes. This house goes back to 1896, did you know that? It was one of the best buildings in the town at one time. But now everybody neglects it. No one paints the door for instance. That door should be painted. And the sheds at the back are a disgrace."

He liked his job in the toilet. "Bums of all shapes and sizes come in there," he said, "and I mean bums. Some of them wash their hands afterwards, some don't. I asked the Council for a radio and they gave me one. Nothing like dance music when you're doing your business. They can even listen to the news. That would give anyone diarrhoea. I sit there and read the *Record* most of the time. There was one day when a woman came in by mistake. Hey, I said, what are you doing here? You never saw anyone so embarrassed." And he laughed his high giggling laugh. "It was like the time I was paid for the milk by this woman who had forgotten to put her teeth in. By golly, she hated herself, she did. And of course some of them who use the toilet don't have much change. I have to find change for them. One of them even offered me a five pound note. He thought I wouldn't charge him, but I did. I found the change. You can't keep up toilets without paying for them. Another day a fellow objected to the soap. Your soap's scented he said. What do you think I am, a poof? Of course it's scented, I said, that's good soap. And, another thing, he said, why don't you have towels, that hot air doesn't dry your hands properly. An old man told me, I get hell from my old woman. I pee on my trousers. There's no force in my pee any more. You really see the world in lavatories."

"That old pervert," said John, "I'll knock his face in."

"He's quite comic," said Linda. "Quieten down. What happened about that electrical job?"

72

"Nothing. It's been filled. There were a hundred and twelve people for it. Imagine that."

"I can believe it. Do you really hate the freezer place?"

"Yes. We never seem to have enough money, do we? I can't even go for a drink with the boys."

"Never mind, your luck will change," said Linda. She was so happy at the prospect of having a baby that her face glowed. That was what she wanted from life, nothing more, a family of children. It was her manifest destiny. She even fantasized about the baby's hair and temper already.

"I hope it won't be like me," said John. "I had a hell of a temper when I was young."

"You still have," said Linda fondly.

"I never slept when I was a baby," said John. "My mother told me that. I was like King Kong."

"Rubbish," said Linda affectionately. "You're a good provider."

"I'll kick his bum in if I see him around you again," said John, whose moustache seemed to vibrate when he was angry. "I will, too."

Cooper would often hoot with laughter. "There was this fellow," he said, "and his pee was deep yellow. He was worried about it too. I had some whisky last night, he said. Do you think it's my liver? Not at all, I said, your liver and your kidneys are two different things. But he was shaking. What whisky was it, I asked him. Black Prince, he said. Oh, that's okay, I told him, that's not so powerful that it will make your pee yellow. That's a nice moderate whisky. Try Tartan next time. The laughs you get! But you get some yobs too. Disgusting. Really filthy. But I won't put up with any of their nonsense. Still you've got to watch. One of them took out a knife one night. I thought I was a goner, but I talked him out of using it. He was blind drunk: maybe he was on drugs."

"He's probably writing all the stuff himself," said John to Linda. "They say that when he was a milkman he had a terrible reputation."

"What do you mean?"

"Well, you know what they say about milkmen. He was giving them more than pints. These sex-starved women. Imagine it. Old Cooper."

And he and Linda laughed. They were young, they were happy, they hadn't been long married. The world was ahead of them. When they woke up in the morning they were excited, anticipatory, confident.

"You should have seen Mrs Floss in her bikini," said John. "She was like a whale. And her skin's dead white."

"Maybe she thinks the back green is the deck of a ship."

"Cooper should marry her. It would be a marriage of convenience." And he laughed out loud. "Get it, marriage of convenience. He works in a toilet, you see. Great. I must tell the boys that."

It was a winter's night, cold and frosty. In December. The street was quiet, as there was an international match between England and Scotland on TV, and Mr Cooper like the rest of the townsmen was watching it. Beside him on the table were six cans of lager. England were winning in spite of the confident forecasts made in the newspapers that this time Scotland would definitely win, as they had Charlie Nicholas. When England scored, Cooper kicked the table on which the cans of lager lay, and went out into the close. He had played football in his youth and still agonized over the international results.

He stood in the close inhaling the air which, though cold, was not unpleasant. He missed the strollers on the street, for in the evening he would stop them and talk to them. He was a gregarious man. He had retired early because of a bad back and still missed his job. Many a time he had seen a strange car parked outside a house. Oh, the things that went on. Milkmen and postmen knew all about them. His own wife had been bedridden for a long while with a heart condition; and he was a full-blooded man.

At that moment, as he stood in the close contemplating

Scotland's latest shame, he heard a scream. It sprang suddenly out of the night and it seemed to him, as he scanned the street, that it had come from the close opposite. It was a high-pitched scream like that made by an animal in a shrubbery or (he recalled) an enemy being bayoneted. He listened and heard it again. Then he saw a man emerging from the close opposite and walking whistling up the street, away from the town. The man was tall and, in the light of the lamp which overhung the close, he saw that there was a scar on his face. The man turned and looked at him and smiled. The smile was a peculiar one, almost conspiratorial, threatening, triumphant. Cooper felt a piercing fear in his bones. Then he heard the scream again.

Without thinking he crossed the street to the close. The lamp cast a yellow foggy light: he didn't like that yellow light much, he preferred the pink one that appeared in the earlier part of the evening. He moved from the stone of the pavement to the stone of the street and then to that of the close. There was nothing to be seen in the close itself. He walked into the back which was darker and only lighted by the illumination from the windows above. Faintly he could hear the noise of the football commentary. He stood there trying to get his eyes accustomed to the blackness. No, it wasn't wholly blackness, there were stripes of yellow: it was like an animal's pelt.

Then he saw a patch of thicker darkness in the corner, and went over towards it. He sniffed. Yes, there was a definite smell of pee, thick and rank. He heard a low moan. He bent down. He felt a coat, a head, a hand. He pulled at the hand and dragged the shape to its feet while it winced and moaned and protested. He was worried for a moment that the person, whoever it was, had been knifed, but there didn't seem to be any blood on his hands: at least they didn't feel sticky. He clasped the hand, pulled the dark mass into the light of the close. The mass dragged its feet, as if it couldn't walk properly. In the light of the lamp that shone sickly above the close, he saw that it was a woman and that she was clad in a dark coat. He dragged her across the street towards his flat which, of course, was on the ground floor. He opened the door and heaved and pushed the woman into a chair, and switched off the television.

He looked down at the woman. Her legs were thin like matchsticks. Her face was pinched and there was blood on her lips where perhaps she had bitten herself. There was a smell of sickness and of pee. The head nodded like a pendulum and he saw to his horror that the woman was a spastic, not a bad one, but a spastic just the same. She must have been about sixty years old. He himself was almost sick, but steadied the woman as she nearly toppled off the chair.

"You okay?" he said.

The woman nodded. She clutched his hand as if she were a child. "Listen," he said, speaking slowly, "I don't know what's happened, but I'm going for the police. Are you sure you're okay?" He left the room and knocked at the Masons' door. But there was no answer: they must be out.

He came back. The woman was still sitting in the chair, her head nodding like that of a marionette.

"Before I go," he said, "you'd better have a drop of whisky." He knew that brandy would be better, but he didn't have any in the house, not since his wife had died. He poured some whisky in a little glass and put it to her lips. She spluttered and tried to get rid of the whisky, but he forced it down her throat.

"It'll do you good," he said. "Take it." She steadied herself and kept some of it down. Her trembling quietened a little.

"Now," he said, again speaking very slowly, "I'm going to phone. I won't be long. I don't have a phone in the house." She signed that she understood. But as her head was nodding all the time anyway, he wasn't sure whether she had understood or not. He walked down the road quickly to the kiosk, which stood at the junction of two streets. He found himself glancing behind him as if he was afraid of the scarred man chasing him. It looked very much as if the scarred man had assaulted the spastic. Imagine it, the very thought was disgusting—and for the first time it occurred to him that perhaps he himself might be under suspicion, be accused. But surely the woman would know that it was he who had rescued her.

He phoned the police and was told they would be along shortly. He walked back. As he did so, he hoped that the woman had not toppled into the electric fire that was burning in front of her. He should have placed her on the sofa, dim fool that he was. He almost ran—so worried he was—but when he arrived the woman was sitting safely in the chair, quite still, staring down at the floor.

"I'll make a cup of tea," he said. "The police won't be long." She didn't say anything, but watched him blankly as he put the kettle on. When he had made the tea he gave her some with plenty of sugar and she steadied a little. As she was drinking it a car drew up at the front of the house, and a policewoman and two men came out. The men were in plain clothes. One was wearing a leather jacket and was tall and heavy with a strong Roman nose and the other was smaller and wore a blue jersey. No one would ever have thought they were policemen. The policewoman came in with them and turned to the spastic.

Suddenly, the spastic spoke for the first time. "It won't be in the papers, will it?"

She had difficulty in speaking. He wondered why this had been the first thing that occurred to her. She had recovered a little and was sitting back in the chair, the centre of attention.

The man with the leather jacket took out a notebook.

"Take your time," he said. "What happened?"

She told him in broken words. She had been visiting a woman in the close opposite Cooper's as she always did on a Thursday evening. As she came down the stairs into the close she was seized and dragged into the back of the close. She screamed and no one heard her, not even the woman she had been visiting. Maybe it was because of the TVs that she hadn't been heard.

The policewoman supported her as she answered the questions. It was in fact the same policewoman as had brought Cooper the news about his wife. She was young and fair-haired. It was, it occurred to him, almost exactly a year before this incident that the policewoman had come to his door, but she had probably forgotten it now. The policewoman had rung the bell and made a cup of tea for him, he remembered that, after she had told him that his wife was dead. He couldn't believe it and had burst out crying. It was the first time that he had cried in his life. His body had been racked by the most tremendous sobs.

The spastic again said that she hoped that this wouldn't get into the papers. The policewoman said that she would now take her down to the station, and then she would run her home in the car. She hadn't seen him at all, the spastic said, he had put his hand on her clothes, but hadn't succeeded . . . Cooper was disgusted. Imagine attacking a spastic. The man must be an animal: worse than an animal.

Eventually he was left with the two policemen in the room where there was a photograph of his wife on the sideboard. She had been young when the photograph was taken and she was wearing a high white collar. There was also a photograph of the two of them with his brother, who had been over from America. That had been some years ago.

The man with the Roman nose introduced himself as Detective Hutton. The one in the blue jersey was called Pierce.

"Now then," said Hutton, "if you could tell us what happened. In your own words. Take your time." Hutton's nose seemed to be sniffing at the air, as if seeking out clues. Pierce smiled at him, a slow genial smile.

"I was watching football," said Cooper, "and I went out."

"Just a moment," Hutton interrupted, "why did you go out?" Pierce smiled, but seemed to approve of the question.

"England had just scored and I was disgusted, so I went out for a breath of fresh air."

"A real fan," said Pierce smiling.

"Yes. The Scottish team is rubbish," said Cooper angrily. "Every year they tell us they're going to win and every year they lose. Why don't they keep their mouths shut?"

"So you went out into the close," said Hutton, "leaving the TV on."

"Yes."

"And?"

"I heard a scream."

"While you were standing in the close?"

"That's right. And then I heard another one."

"I see. And?"

"And then I saw," Cooper concentrated, "a fellow coming out of the close and walking up the street."

"Which direction?" said Pierce in his soft voice.

"Away from the town. Towards the council houses."

"So," said Hutton, "Did you recognize him?"

"No, I didn't recognize him. But I would know him again."

Immediately he had spoken Cooper wished he hadn't been so definite. After all if he interfered in his affairs, this man might do him. Or his relatives might. Then again he might have to attend an official identification parade. Still he repeated, "I would recognize him."

"Good," said Pierce. His lips set like a trap and for the first time Cooper realized that Pierce was the more dangerous man of the two policemen, the harder. He had heard stories of policemen, of course. Why, they might beat you up for no reason in the secrecy of the station.

"He had a scar on his face," he said slowly.

"Ah," said Pierce, looking at Hutton. "Which side of his face was towards you?"

"The left. No, the right," said Cooper. "He was whistling and smiling. He smiled across at me." He shivered.

"MacDowell," said Pierce quickly to Hutton.

"Our friend," said Hutton.

"Just out of prison, too," said Pierce meditatively. "Bloody fool. He can't leave it in his trousers."

Cooper gazed at the picture of his wife on the sideboard. If it had been her. If it had been Flora being attacked there in the darkness. And screaming. Sometimes she had screamed with the pain when she had been in the house, but never in the hospital. He hadn't realized that she would go so quickly. Her temperament had been marvellous: she was resigned to her death. Sometimes she would smile at passers-by out of the low window. Latterly she didn't speak much. Of course she had always been shy, much shyer than he was. There was always a nice gentle air about her.

Suddenly, for no reason he said, "I was in the war, you know. We used to clear out houses when we entered a town. You never knew whether there were Germans there or not. You often threw a grenade in."

"Oh," said Pierce, "neither of us was in the war."

There was a silence. "There was this German and I had to bayonet him," said Cooper. "He was big and fat and he wore glasses. He was just about to throw a grenade. It was him or me."

"Yes," said Pierce, "of course."

Naturally neither of them had been in the war: they were too young. It seemed to him that they too were like animals, on the scent: their nostrils twitched when they heard about the scar.

"Will I have to go to court?" he asked.

"Well," said Pierce, "you might. Does that bother you? Sometimes they plead guilty. MacDowell is not all there anyway." And he tapped his forehead.

Animal, thought Cooper. Imagine trying to rape a spastic in a dark close. He must have realized that she was spastic and left. Or perhaps he hadn't. Maybe she had resisted so hard that he had given up. Straight out of prison and back into it again. What stupidity, what unassailable stupidity. But it was the smile that troubled him. The smile had crossed the road and had communicated with him. It was as if it was insinuating, "You say anything about this and I'll get you". It was like that man who had emerged out of Jenny Dickson's house, tightening his belt on a May morning long ago. Her husband of course worked away from home: he had wondered whether he should tell him, send him an anonymous note. He had been standing there with the white milk bottle in his hand. From inside the house he could hear the crying of a child. It had been a beautiful morning with the mist beginning to clear and the waters of the loch flat calm, every shadow clearly defined. These mornings on his milk round, how miraculously pure some of them had been.

"One other thing," said Pierce, "how good is the light?"

"What do you mean?"

"The light across the road? Could you see him clearly? There's a bit of a fog tonight. I wonder if you would . . ."

"What?"

"If you would do something for us. Could you walk across the road and come out of the close and smile at us and then walk up the street?"

"Why?" said Cooper. He suddenly felt afraid. Did they think he had done it? What if the woman accused him? Before she left, the spastic had said, "Mrs Snow will never speak to me again. I just know it. She won't have me back in the house."

He realized, however, that he must do what they asked him to do: otherwise they might suspect him.

"Okay," he said. He walked across the road and into the close. Then he came out, straightened his shoulders as he skirted the orbit of the lamp that was bent over the close, like a scholar perusing the stone. He began to whistle, but his lips were too dry for him to do so easily. He nearly shouted over to the two policemen, "I can't whistle." He tried his hardest but all that came out of his mouth was a dry sound. He made himself walk jauntily with the posture of a man who has nothing to lose, nothing to gain, who has no future. He smiled over at Pierce who was standing in the door of his close like an obscure reflection of himself. He imagined a scar on his cheek and nearly put up his finger to touch it. Had the scar been left by a knife wound in a fight? He couldn't imagine MacDowell's life in and out of prison, squabbling, defending himself. Also he had been told that he was rather simple: he himself didn't feel simple at all. On the contrary, he felt the complexity of the situation. After he had walked up the street he came to a halt. For a moment there it was as if he intended to continue to walk away from his own close, as if he didn't intend to return to the complex world of notebook and interrogation.

Pierce was waiting for him at the door.

"Yes," he said quietly, "I could see you clearly enough." And he smiled genially at Cooper. "You did a good job. You looked exactly as he might have looked."

"That's right," said Hutton, "I was thinking that we can establish the time quite easily if it was just when England scored."

Damn England, Cooper thought. They were always beating us and for the moment in his anger he forgot himself, the possible danger he was in. Nothing but failure, loss. He shivered, feeling the cold for the first time.

"You should have a whisky," said Pierce. "Do you have any?"

Cooper pointed to the bottle that was still lying on the sideboard. Some detective! "I gave her some," he said.

"Oh," said Pierce.

"And tea as well. After I had come back from phoning. I didn't want to leave her alone, but my next door neighbours weren't in when I knocked."

"Good," said Pierce. "You did very well." It was as if he was being decorated. "You did very well indeed. Not many people would have kept their heads as you did. And the street was deserted?"

"Yes, because of the match."

"Of course," said Pierce.

The two detectives got to their feet. "Well, that's enough. If I were you I would have a whisky and a rest," said Pierce. "We'll sort him out."

They left the room and went into their car. They turned it in the direction of the council house scheme. They waved. Cooper waved back. After they had gone he sat down but he didn't turn on the TV. England would win anyway. He knew that in his bones.

He remembered the day he had last gone to visit his wife. She had been in an oxygen tent and had smiled at him. The surgeon had said, "No immediate danger."

"I'll be back as usual tonight," said Cooper.

And then the policewoman had come to the door. He had heard the doorbell. It was late and the night was dark and frosty. Who was this? He wasn't expecting anyone. And the policewoman had stood there. And she had told him that Flora had died. There was snow on her coat like a sparkle of fading diamonds. She was quite young with a cold sore on her lip. She took off her diced cap and laid it beside her on the sofa. And then he had cried and cried.

Sometimes his wife would say to him, "I don't know why you are always talking to that Linda. Every time she goes for coal you're out there talking to her."

"Well, she's friendly. And you know I like talking to people." And Flora would hear from her becalmed chair the sound of his high voice laughing. Linda could take a good joke. You could even tell her dirty jokes which you couldn't tell your wife. And furthermore, she was Catholic and there was that one about the nun and the population problem . . .

The policewoman had sat down opposite him. He thought that she was acting towards him as if he were an old man long extinct. And he was shaking, no doubt about it. He had to take his cup in both hands to steady him and warm him at the same time.

It was December the 27th, he remembered that clearly. Between Christmas and New Year.

The policewoman had blonde hair, like a helmet of gold.

"Will you be all right?" she was saying. "Are you sure you will be all right?"

"I'll be all right," he kept saying. And then, "I don't understand it. The surgeon said that there was no immediate danger. She was smiling."

"These things can happen," said the policewoman. "Anyway it may have been a blessing. Was she in much pain?"

"Sometimes. But not much at the hospital."

He was overwhelmed by memories. There was their marriage: then their honeymoon in Brighton. Then the years together. Of course they never had any children and that was a tragedy: he didn't believe it was anything to do with him. She liked children and so did he: but nothing ever happened. They had talked of adopting a child, but nothing had come of it. Of course as a milkman he didn't have a huge salary.

When they were young they used to drive out into the country in the car. One day they saw a weasel. It had turned and looked at them ferociously as if to say "I am not frightened of you". Their car in those days was a yellow Mini.

The policewoman crossed her legs negligently. She leaned over him with her cup of tea. She was so young, so pretty, so hopeful. She'd probably just started her job.

And then the terrible thing happened, the extraordinary thing, the awful thing. He had watched her legs, following the curve of her thighs. He couldn't believe it. Was he some sort of blind uncaring animal? He would have taken that policewoman if she had offered herself to him. And this just after his wife's death. Was he some kind of monster? He stared fixedly at the sweet flesh. Oh God, such piercing desire he felt: it was almost like pain.

As if the policewoman was conscious of what was happening she uncrossed her legs and got to her feet. He himself ran to the bathroom and was violently sick. The yellow stuff spurted from his mouth all over the floor which had linoleum on it. After he had been sick, he was okay again. Beast that I am, he thought, as he saw her to the door. The stars were bright in the sky, millions of them, twinkling in the frost. He never saw the policewoman again till tonight.

He did have a scar, he said to himself. And I'll get him for it. I'm not frightened. It was as if the man had raped his own wife in the dark close. Animal he thought. Smiler. Beast. Monster. Sex-maniac.

THE WALLS OF the old tenement sweated. The flaky paint on the door was green and scarred. Drunks vomited in the close as they staggered home at midnight and after. Perhaps the spirit of the old matron was still pottering about with its brush, flicking at dust and crisp-papers. The matron, old and grey-haired, spoke little: she had dusted round the bins every morning. One of these days, John Mason would say, she will put up notices. There had hardly ever been any children in the tenement except for Mrs Miller's two girls and boy whom the matron had disliked because they insisted on sliding down the bannisters shouting war cries. Now, however, there would be Linda's child and the tenement would blossom again briefly as it had done before. Of course in the distant past there would have been large families.

When the matron died the flat had been empty for six months, and mice had infested the building. The Masons and the Porters had put down traps all the time and then Mr Cooper's stray cat had killed most of them: a bonanza of grey flesh. However, one day Mr Cooper had found the cat dead outside his door. It had been run down by a big lorry, flattened, like a leaf.

The old pipes squeaked. Workmen left their footsteps in the wet cement and the matron became angry with them. Mrs Brown went to visit her husband's grave in the neatly kept cemetery with its locked doors. He had died of an embolism. On his grave she placed flowers which she had grown in the back green. Sometimes the glass jar in the cemetery shook, and collapsed in the wind. If it was a good day, she might walk back from the cemetery in her black clothes.

Who had lived in that tenement? Lord knew there had been so many. Workers, professional men, housewives. Clothes had hung on the line, patched, poor. Knickers had ballooned outwards in a spring wind and had then faded away like clouds. The history of changing society could be learned from the tenement. Furniture changed, wallpaper changed, so did clothes.

Sometimes at night Mrs Floss thought she heard voices in the walls as of newly wed couples swearing eternal allegiance to each other. How many coats of paint had the walls known, how many sheaves of wallpaper; from the coloured to the plain? Linoleum gave way to carpets, old white cracked basins to warm coloured suites. The tenement swung to the wheel and wind of history. Tall and gaunt it stood in the storms, windows rattled, were swung out like sails on creaking ropes. Women hung above the streets with mops in their hands. Coalmen bent like dwarfs under dirty sacks.

The matron prodded with her broom as if investigating a disease. Faintly from far streets the voices of children could be heard. Mrs Miller lay on her bed in her fur coat while the whitewash flaked from the ceiling. She dreamt of Rhodesia, the matron dreamt of her days and nights in hospital, dressed in her brief authority. The tenement was a well of voices, whispering, shouting.

Mrs Floss bought a sideboard and wasn't satisfied and bought another one. She laid a carpet and was dissatisfied and bought another one. Why had she taken a flat here? She could have gone elsewhere, she had plenty of money, why was she involved in constant renovation? But the flat was central and she couldn't drive. One day she had asked John, Linda's husband, if he would run her to the hospital where she was getting treatment, probably for alcoholism. He had set her down and waited for her. Later, much later, she wandered out of the hospital shouting, "Jimmy, where are you Jimmy?" Then she had asked if he would stop at the Co-op and wait for her while she bought some messages. She treated him like a servant and he accepted it all good-humouredly. She was a card, the old girl. He always remembered her in later years as standing in the sunshine outside the hospital and shouting, "Where are you, Jimmy?" Indubitably half drunk. A pale, old drunken face glimmered at a window.

Mrs Brown would examine the bottles in the bin and say to Linda, "That woman, Mrs Floss, drinks a lot. See all these whisky bottles and sherry bottles. Disgusting." She maintained that Mrs Floss put her empties in her bin, but Linda reckoned that they were Mrs Brown's own. Who would have thought that she drank too?

Trevor Porter brooded over his poems. Dante's head burned above the tenement like the morning star. His verses were like the bars of the raw electric fire, wounded, scarred.

The wind played about the tenement on March days. It spun papers, in dizzy circles, rings. Mrs Miller looked out at the sky on a stormy night while the blue lightning quivered. Let it hit someone else, she prayed. Trevor Porter once saw it at the tips of his fingers when he was typing.

The unmentionable things that go on over there, Mrs Brown would say to the matron, peering across to the opposite side of the street. Prostitution is rife, she would say in a whisper, her eyes gleaming. Girls with short flame-coloured skirts were seen leaving the flats regularly. There was music from feral records on hot summer nights.

Would you believe it, the matron would say, seeing the Red Indians pass. The colours of their hair were exotic, mediaeval. It was as if the town had been taken over by invaders from outer space. Hell's Angels in leather jackets careered up and down the street after midnight. "I do not want to give my name," she would say on the phone to the police, "but really . . ." Invariably when the police arrived the street was quiet again. These black alien riders seemed to have a sixth sense for trouble. In their visors and masks.

Trevor wrote a poem which went as follows:

Someone is saying "I'll knife you, son,"
just below my window in the night.

What is this. A Midsummer Night's Dream,
a remarkable inflection of the light.

A shudder as of fear, of ecstasy.
Shakespeare's scavenging magnificent mind
hovering in a blue Elizabethan sky,
learning the killer's lingo in the wind.

"I'll knife you, son," he said. That firm quiet voice
assertive for a moment. Let me see—
Lear is struggling through the wind and gorse
in the spiky crown of his senility.

That shudder once again. That betrayal . . .
I pull the curtains wide. The moon is full.
And somewhere in the night the parched beasts prowl
in the dense shrubberies beyond our rule.

One day Mrs Floss, who was slightly drunk, took her brother
into the Porters' flat, having found the door open.

"This," she told him, "is their lobby. Notice the nice carpet.
And this is the kitchen, roomy isn't it? Now here is Mr Porter,
typing. Good morning, Mr Porter." Trevor gazed at her in
amazement. "Mrs Porter collects these figures. Beautiful, aren't
they?"

And so she proceeded on her guided tour through the flat,
saying goodbye to Trevor as she left. He didn't think Julia had
been in that day. She laughed and laughed when she heard of
Mrs Floss's safari, and especially at Mrs Floss's indication to her
brother,

"And there is Mr Porter, typing."

Mrs Floss's husband had owned an hotel in the town.
Latterly, he had given up bothering with it and read books
instead. Mrs Floss served in the bar and had done so for years.
Her husband was a thin man who had grown shyer as the years
passed: he always wore a carnation in his buttonhole. He would
have sold the hotel if it hadn't been for his wife. He would go to

the library and ask Mrs Stewart for the latest books which he had seen reviewed in the *Observer*, and the *Sunday Times*. She hated the sight of him: he gave her more work than all her other customers combined. He was always making her fill in forms ordering books from the Central Library, as he had started to take a keen interest in history, especially the history of the town.

Mrs Floss had been unfaithful to him many times with men whom she had met in the bar. Once, too, with a Spaniard whom she met while she was on holiday on her own, as her husband refused to visit the hot countries ever since he had had his stomach-upset. "You go," he would say to her. "Your brother can run the hotel while you're gone." She always went in the late season when the fares were low and the cities were not crowded.

Her longest affair was with a policeman whose wife had eventually left him. Her friendship with the policeman was useful to her, as she could keep the hotel open later than normal and she earned other perquisites. The policeman was a big man who despised Mr Floss: he himself never read books and was not very popular in the town, as he was always arresting people for trivial offences. The two of them, Mrs Floss and he, often made love in the police van, which appealed to her romantic nature. Mr Floss knew that this was going on, but as he had been impotent for years he didn't care.

"I don't understand what you see in him," he would say mildly. "He seems to me to be a lout." She thought if he were a real man he would fight for her, but of course her husband never dreamed of doing that. He knew that he would lose anyway. He had long ago lost respect for his wife and was happy with his books. He had inherited the hotel and had never liked running it: it was too much like advertising soap.

"If you don't watch out," she would say to him, "we will be bankrupt. Do you realize that most people are now bringing caravans to the area and also taking self-service flats? Petrol, too, has gone up in price and people want the good weather: they will go to the Continent rather than here. The other thing is, you'd better make sure that you have proper fire precautions. They are going to be very strict on that."

"Maybe we should set the place on fire, and cash the insurance money," her husband said mildly. She had not been too horrified at the idea, but knew that he was only joking. In fact there had been a big fire in a neighbouring hotel in which three visitors had died. It had been started by a porter throwing a burning cigarette-end into a waste paper basket. About that time there had been an epidemic of fires in the town, one of which had gutted the cinema. It had been rebuilt and was now used for bingo.

Her most satisfactory romance had been with an Italian she had met in Venice. They had spent a splendid month together sailing in gondolas, visiting magnificent houses and theatres. She had thought Venice absolutely divine. Everything was so romantic, especially the moonlight on the waters which during the day looked rather dirty. The sun blazed down from a perfectly blue sky every day, the pigeons were a blizzard in the famous square of St Mark, the clock-tower with its soldiers was so unusual. The Italian too was very attentive, but he didn't pay for anything. Still, she didn't mind that: she didn't mind the heat either. She returned home to find that Alex had had a stroke: he gibbered to her in a strange broken language. He lasted for two months before the second stroke hit him and killed him outright.

It was quite amazing how badly she took his death. When he was alive she hadn't bothered about him, now that he was dead she remembered his kind nature. She wept continually and stopped seeing the policeman. She burnt the letters she had received from the Italian. Indeed, she had a tremendous bout of burning and putting out. It was as if she wished to be rid of her old life in order to clear the decks for her new one. She dressed in sober clothes, decided to sell the hotel. She couldn't bear to be in the bar listening to the usual chatter which she had heard so often before. She looked around for a flat and eventually found the one she was in. Her sons, who were grown up, sometimes visited her and once when she was away they stole her carpet, and sold it. Mr Cooper had tried to stop them after he had seen them at midnight, walking down the stair with it, but they called him an old interfering fart and he had popped into his flat again like a cuckoo on a clock.

She got a large amount of money for the hotel and began to drink heavily. She went on a world cruise and dozed on the deck of a huge liner for weeks. She had an affair with a steward who came from Liverpool and who was a sad descent from her bronzed Italian and Spaniard. In fact, he had a harelip and a liking for pink gin. She found that when she came to writing postcards she knew of no one she wanted to send them to. When she arrived home she had her hair done and then changed all the furniture in the flat again. She would try to keep the workers in the flat as long as possible by offering them drink. She found the loneliness oppressive and nearly went out of her mind as she had no inner resources to fall back on. She never read a book. Once she nearly put her flat on fire while trying to cook chips. The flex of the cooker burnt out and she couldn't operate the fire extinguisher which she had bought. She poured water over the flames but they shot up higher than ever. John Mason had explained to her the use of salt in situations like that, but she forgot in the middle of the crisis.

She went to bed late and woke late. Sometimes she would wander about the lobby in her nightgown with her teeth out. For no reason at all she would begin to think about her dead husband, whom she now idolized, remembering his gentle forgetful ways. At the same time she missed her lovers; she had become fat and rather ugly and she knew it. She didn't have any mirrors in the flat. One of her sons took to drugs (he was the leader in removing her carpet). When she went away she would not know who to leave the key with, but eventually left it with Mrs Porter with whom she used to have a coffee; and then of course Mrs Porter didn't know anything of her previous life. She was a nice woman, unhappy, but who wasn't? She said that she wanted more than anything to leave the flat and find a house preferably in Devon. But her husband wanted to stay in Scotland because he wrote poetry, though she couldn't understand why you couldn't write poetry anywhere. All she knew about poetry was that there was little money in it. Mrs Porter was a brave woman; she didn't want her husband to know that she had cancer.

She discussed the light on the stair with Mr Porter. Actually he didn't give a damn, she could tell that, but she wanted someone to talk to. Mr Porter, she thought, was rather snooty and despised her if that was not too strong a word. She thought he was rather like Alex, but not so kind: there was a remoteness about him. He was a funny little man who wore a crushed hat, summer and winter. He also had a cat and she didn't like cats: she much preferred dogs. Dogs were friendlier animals. In fact she thought she might get one: you never knew where you were with a cat. Cats were hypocrites, they gave you only cupboard love. Dogs were true friends. She did in fact buy a big black dog but Mr Cooper must have told someone about it and she had to give it up. She thought Mr Porter more of a gentleman than Mr Cooper.

She hated what she was becoming. In the hotel, once, there had been a maid who had been about forty years old. The maid stayed in the attic room in the summer, and had no friends. She used to go to church every Sunday and on Wednesday nights as well. She bought a lot of pamphlets about God which asked whether you were saved or not. She was thin and wore glasses and was very conscientious. But in spite of that the customers didn't like her, thought her too spiritual. She had always found that. The ones the customers liked the best were the harum-scarum negligent good-looking ones, the ones she couldn't depend on. A pretty face went a long way. She herself had been pretty in her youth, but now she didn't dare look in the mirror.

Sometimes she would go on diets, but found that she couldn't keep to them. She ate cakes and of course she drank a lot of vodka and gin and this put on calories. She ate many sweets. She had read in some newspaper that over-eating was a compensation for unhappiness.

She tried to make friends with Mr Porter, inviting him to watch TV programmes, but he never came. He was a queer cold fish. Mrs Porter had told her that he sometimes spent hours in his room typing, not speaking to her. What a life. Of course Alex had been much the same. He should never have married. He was too good for her, he should have been a saint. She should have married a farmer, a big strong man with natural desires. Once she had gone to a fortune teller who had first of all asked her for a cigarette and then told her that there was going to be a big romance in her life. She had asked for another cigarette at the end of the reading. Mrs Floss gave her the whole packet wondering how a fortune teller couldn't afford cigarettes of her own. But of course there had been no romance. Poor Alex, what a life she had led him, what a dance. How he must have suffered! Now that she was suffering she realized what he must have suffered too. Imagine what she had been like. Prettifying herself for that policeman while Alex knew exactly what was happening. No wonder she drank, remembering that.

She had also made attempts to make friends with Mrs Miller. The two of them could even drink together. But Mrs Miller wouldn't let anyone into her flat and she stank as well in these unmentionable furs, and she went with men who lived in caves. No, Mrs Miller wasn't respectable, and neither were her friends. She quite liked the Masons, especially John who had driven her to the hospital once or twice when she had her dizzy spells. He looked like an Italian or a Spaniard and had a handsome moustache. Linda she kept at a distance, because she sensed that the latter disapproved of her. John perhaps disapproved of her as well, as his own father was an alcoholic who came to the house and made trouble even when Linda was pregnant. She had heard that John had knocked his own father down.

Sometimes she would get letters of Mr Porter's by mistake, for the postman was rather careless. She would open the letters without looking at the address. Once she went in and handed

Mr Porter a letter addressed to him, which she had inadvertently opened, and he was angry. He didn't say much but she could tell that he was seething. That bloody woman, he would be thinking to himself. Actually it had been from a magazine and it had been the return of a poem. So that's to you, old fart, she muttered under her breath. Anyone would think that she wasn't a human being. Of course she should never have opened the letter, but most gentlemen would have accepted her apology with good grace.

She dreamed that she and Mr Porter would get married and she would be no longer on her own. She would move into his flat which was much bigger than her own. Maybe some day Mr Porter would become famous and she would travel with him all over the world. But she didn't think that he would become famous, not like Catherine Cookson. Still she would not be alone. Loneliness was a disease, worse than a disease, it was a living death. It ate into one. Nights she thought that she would scream out loud. She felt imprisoned, in solitary confinement. She had been sentenced and condemned by an invincible destiny which was laughing at her. Maybe she ought to go to church but she didn't want to do that. She couldn't remember when she had been in church last and she didn't like the thought of it. It was an affair of stained glass windows, middle-aged women with hymn books, a silly minister and a cross. The church hadn't helped her when Alex died. No one had helped her then, no one. She had stared down at his cold tranquil scholarly face which was as if carved from stone. She hardly recognized him, he looked so boyish, so austere. Her brother had to organize the funeral for her. She remembered the undertaker, very correct in his black tie and black jacket. He had been in his own way a very humane man, had even tried to tell jokes. He had told her a joke about a worker of his who had been hit by the fist of a corpse jerking into rigor mortis.

"What did you do that for?" the worker had shouted, "I didn't do anything to you." He had been trying to calm her down for she was in hysterics. She had thought that the end of the world had come, that she would never recover. It had taken all her strength to sell the hotel and move into this flat which she now didn't like. But she didn't want to move again. There were no children here, there was an air of decay, people had come to their last resting place, it was like a grave.

"I didn't notice that address," she said to Mr Porter. But he had stared at her and taken that letter without a word. Later, she had passed him on the stair and he had ignored her. Once he had locked himself out, he wasn't very practical. Strangely enough she hadn't done that yet, though she probably would. It was her husband who had filled in the forms to do with the hotel and dealt with the accounts. When he died she found that she didn't understand what was happening. While she was having her affairs he had been shoring up the place. The lawyer, however, with whom she had slept many years before, had kept her right. Monstrous. She had been a monster. But she had always had a strong sexual drive and he hadn't. He always thought sex dirty. He preferred his books.

It was awful being in a single bed night after night especially in summer, when the tenement was really hot. Below her window she could hear the voices of lovers as they strolled past and, with a bitterness that she could not believe possible, they reminded her of her lost youth. She would flutter about the flat in her nightgown like a lost butterfly blinded by light, beating against an invisible panel of glass. The broken narratives she heard intrigued her, excited her.

One night when she was drunk she had rung the bell of Mr Porter's door (his wife's name had been removed).

"I wanted to tell you," she said, "that your wife was a very unhappy woman."

"Is that all you wanted to tell me," he said.

"You think you're better than me. But she told me you used to have trouble with your classes."

"Oh?"

"We used to have coffee together. You didn't know about

that, did you? She told me that you and your son didn't get on."

All she could see was a tightening of Mr Porter's lips. The poison poured out of her, but she couldn't stop herself.

"He never comes to see you," she said.

"He was here about a week ago," said Mr Porter, "if it interests you."

At least this drunken aggressive conversation was better than silence.

"She told me he never came to see you. You weren't on the same wavelength," she said. And Mrs Floss swayed in the lobby, almost falling down.

"And another thing, I asked my boys. They didn't like you in the school."

Mr Porter said nothing, but slammed the door in her face. She was about to strike on it with her naked fist, but decided against it. God damn him, who did he think he was with his air of superiority! Were we not all human? The door was a flat wooden wall. The holes where the nails had been for the nameplates showing Mrs Porter's name winked at her in the light. She nearly screamed at him, "You old bastard". But there was a deep silence everywhere.

When she went back in she lay on her bed and wept. What sort of woman was she becoming? She hated herself. Alex, Alex, she cried, beating on the pillow with her fists. But there was no answer. Alex was dead. Everyone was dead. Only she was alive. Alex was happy, she was not.

But there was one thing that unlike Mrs Miller she wouldn't do. She would never go into the town on her own and drink. If she drank she drank in the house. She had enough pride and dignity to do that.

One day a Jehovah's Witness came to the door. He was a middle-aged man and he worked on the roads.

"Are you saved?" he asked her. She didn't know what to say. He kept her talking for more than an hour. She had invited him in but he wouldn't come in. He referred to texts from the Bible, naming them by chapter and verse. He really must be a clever man, though he only worked on the roads. He was most eloquent and sometimes seemed to speak with a voice that was not his own. She had seen him drinking tea by himself in the station buffet.

"If we are not saved by Jesus, what are we?" he said. "Some people think we come from apes, that's what they call the Darwinian theory, but no one can believe that really. We were created by God in his own image in the Garden of Eden, see Genesis. Don't you believe that?"

"What can we do about loneliness?" she asked him. His eyes shifted. "Put yourself in the hands of God," he said. "That is all we can do." Eventually on his sixth visit he did come into the house and they had a gin. "Not, mind you, that I'm a drinker but a little wine for thy stomach's sake."

She looked forward to his visits. He seemed to have all the time in the world to talk to her. He brought her a *Watchtower* which she used for lighting the fire, though the paper wasn't all that good quality.

She knew that he was from the town and that he knew all about her previous history. He could have known Alex too. Latterly Alex would sit by the fire watching TV. The first stroke had only affected his legs, not his speech. One night he had started to cry helplessly and couldn't stop himself. It had been awful, appalling.

"You're married?" she said to the Jehovah's Witness.

"Yes, happily married. The condition of wedlock is a blessed one. Without a companion what are we in this world? But Jesus too is our wife, our husband, Jesus too helps us as a spouse would, more than a spouse would."

"Does he wash the dishes?" she nearly asked him.

He was a funny man. He was a roadsweeper, she had seen him on the street in the early morning with his brush and his metal cart.

One night when she was drunk she shouted at him, "All you come here for is my money. You're an old hypocrite. My son told me about you. He takes drugs and has been to India. I wanted him to become a lawyer, but he didn't want to. First of all he drove a taxi and then he got a girl into trouble. I can't do anything with him. But he told me about you. You used to drink a lot yourself."

"That is indeed true. I was an alcoholic, but I found the Lord. He showed me the correct path. You should do the same." His voice was insufferably mild like Alex's: nothing she said to him offended him.

"Money is everything," she said. "If I was poor I would be even worse off. I wouldn't have a flat. I know that."

"God said that the meek shall inherit the earth. Look what happened to Dives, the rich man." He spoke like a clock that had been wound up. Like one of those robots that she had once bought Stewart for a toy.

Eventually she slammed the door in his face, and drank a huge glass of vodka. He never came again. And when she passed him in the road, he would bow his head like Jesus on the cross.

Tinkers, too, would come to the door asking for rags, and she would give them good clothes. A tramp came and asked her if she wanted any knives or other instruments sharpened. Apart from that she had few visitors.

She used to watch the TV a lot, but she had gone off that too. She became fed up with Morecambe and Wise and the Two Ronnies. The only films she really liked were horror ones but as they were on late at night and she was alone in the house, she thought twice about watching them. She had to take a lot of drink to tolerate the fear, but the difficulty was that then she couldn't see the screen very well. One of the horror films really terrified her. It was about a couple touring in a caravan who found themselves the victims of a Black Mass ceremony. Even the local minister was involved. The caravan was eventually ringed with mad addicts of the devil, while the faces of the man and wife looked out pale as chalk, as paper. That night she had an awful dream. Alex's face was peering out of a caravan which was going on fire. Alex had been cremated, that was what he had wanted. She herself would be buried. Alex's face was burning, the flesh was melting on it, and she was shouting as the curtains hissed and crackled. "We'll go bankrupt. The tourists are bringing their own caravans." It seemed to her that the tenement was full of voices, clawed hands reached for her. Bony fingers. Oh, God, I can't bear any more, she would say, putting her fingers in her ears. But she did bear more and more. She had to. In the mornings she slept late. In the light of day, the world didn't look so bad. She went to Barrets' and ordered a new sideboard.

Her world would be like this for ever. She would pay for her sins, deceiving Alex. Her friends had been hypocritical, they had been waiting patiently for her downfall. The day that Alex had been cremated was in April. The ground flickered with shadow and light. The coffin slid into an inferno of flame. He winked at her, holding a book in his hand. The book burned leaf by leaf. And his face became vague as he, burning, read the burning book.

"Please give this to the baby," she said to Linda one day. It was a beautiful white shawl which she had been given for Stewart, her first born. "Please take it."

"Yes," said Linda, "thank you. How beautiful, how really beautiful. Thank you very much."

TREVOR STUDIED THE diary day after day. It went back to his time in the war. It talked of his father, but not him, playing with Robin.

"My jealousy is great," she wrote at one point. "Why is that?" She was referring to one night when that woman Lydia Lawson had visited them.

"You talked about education all night," she had said to Trevor. "You never referred to me. Of course I was only a secretary. Is that it?"

"It never occurred to me that you felt like that," said Trevor. As usual he was helpless before her. Her mind was keener, quicker than his. He had met her in his first school. She was young, fresh, enthusiastic. She had come to Scotland because she had read about the country as a girl and also, if the truth be told, to set some distance between herself and her mother. But latterly she began to miss Devon. She and Robin would sometimes go to the farm on holiday. The ducks with their proud red masks would strut past them: the hens would pick at the corn: and the pigs wallowed in a great grey ocean of their own. Trevor thought that perhaps he should apply for a small undemanding school in Devon. But he knew that he would miss the city, the town: he was an urbanite by nature.

All these days he had underestimated Julia. Because he was a poet he had thought her in some way inferior: he was an unconscious élitist. But in fact she was more intelligent than him, more acute in seizing the essentials of a practical problem and solving it. And now he was discovering her secret life that had been hidden from him.

Love, what was it? Often at night she would say, "Do you love me?" And he had never been able to say the words. Why was that? Some deep instinct, spare and Puritan, had kept his lips shut. And yet he had loved his wife. Now he knew it. She had held his life together. And she had been so brave at the end, keeping from him exactly what was wrong with her, though of course he suspected. "Are you in pain?" he would say to her.

"No, I'm not in pain." And yet she must have been. The crab had been gnawing at her. The outlaw restless cells had been proliferating.

She had bought a lot of plants for the house. These were her substitute for a garden. She was more superstitious than him, and had even spoken to the plants. She had a strange theory about the afterlife: she didn't believe that either of them would die. She believed that when Jesus said, "In my father's house are many mansions", he had meant that the mansions were planets, arranged in a special order. To the best planets the perfected spirits migrated. Trevor himself had no belief in an afterlife. On the contrary, he believed that, when one died, that was the end. He would never meet Julia again. And this bothered him; and made him feel an ultimate desolation.

I am Robinson Crusoe on his island, he thought. There is desert, sand, all about me. I have to begin again, rebuild. He began to paint the walls and the doors and the sills of the windows and the ceilings. He bought huge cans of green paint. He wanted to start again but something was preventing him. The Camerons haunted him. He felt he should have confronted Cameron while Julia was still alive. But he had been too frightened. Now, he didn't want to move because he felt that by doing so he would have taken advantage of Julia. He must suffer like her, to the end.

"You should do something about Mrs Cameron," Julia had often said to him.

"What can I do? It's none of our business. Even the police won't interfere unless she charges him."

"But she won't do it. Where can she go?"

"Well, I can't do anything about it."

He had cringed away from all decisions, leaving them in the end to her. At times he felt that he should leave the flat and go on some sort of tour. At other times he was tempted to drink heavily. But he did neither of these things. On the contrary he spent part of his time in doing crosswords, puzzles. He remembered their Sundays together when he would tackle the Azed crossword in the *Observer*.

"Is there a word 'pavis'?" he would say. "It means a shield for the whole body."

"How should I know," she would say, looking up from her knitting.

And then again, "Is there a word 'paxwax'?" Then he would say, "This is a brilliant man, Azed." And she would answer without looking up from her knitting (she was always knitting things for her grand-daughter), "You're only saying that because you've solved the crossword." He would spend hours on the Azed crossword as if it was the most important thing in the world. But he would never try to solve the puzzles presented by their daily lives.

One day they had stood at the window watching a wedding. The bride was in white and her husband stood beside her. The photographer was bending down as if about to shoot. The taxi, like a hearse loaded with flowers, was ready. Tired women stood at the wall staring at the bride with envious eyes. That too had been the greatest day of their lives, the only day when they had been the centre of attention. The wind blew the bride's gown about. The husband nearly always had a suit that didn't quite fit him. The minister held up a benevolent hand. Julia loved weddings, christenings. She had looked forward with so much eagerness to the birth of their grandchild: Trevor hadn't. He hadn't realized how much the birth had meant to her. But then his son was in Cambridge, and he was here.

Robin came to visit him again and they had a cup of coffee, in the huge kitchen, out of two mugs, one of which had Taurus inscribed on it, the other Capricorn. (Capricorn was the goat who lived frugally, was determined to attain its purpose, was mean and persistent. Taurus was the fleshly one who loved comfort, the sensual flesh.)

"Everything okay?" said Robin again. It was clear that he was visiting his father from a sense of duty and would rather have been elsewhere.

"Fine," said Trevor. They drank their coffee in silence. Trevor didn't want to talk about intimate family things. He asked his son about computers: would they take over from men? Did they have a single-minded evil intelligence? Would they be able to write *King Lear?*

"Of course not," said Robin, laughing. Trevor glanced at him. This was his son telling him about a new world, a world that he himself didn't understand, Robin was happy among his computers because his emotions had been amputated. He had turned away from the world of literature to that of mathematics, where everything remained constant, unchanging. His father belonged to the age of the dinosaur as far as he was concerned.

His son had never been able to look on him as a father. He had never come to him with his problems, only to his mother. How can I be a poet, Trevor asked himself, if I am not a human being? If I am a coward in life, will I not be a coward in poetry as well? There is a deep connection between all aspects of life. Was even his poetry programmed by his innate cowardice without his knowing it?

There was something he wished to say to his son. He wished to say, "I know my faults now. Is it too late to remedy them?" His stair-woman had talked about selfishness. Was he not the selfish one? Was there anyone more selfish than the artist? Did he not have blood on his hands daily? He existed in the world of reflection while others dealt with the real world. Others had sensed that his poetry was not real, that in a fundamental way he despised his reader: they sensed his lack of humanity. Was that not the root of his problem? After all, if he could not talk to his son, how could he reach the invisible reader who also was composed of blood and bones? All his life the U-boats had been waiting to attack, following him beneath the surface of the sea. And he was intensely vulnerable.

"Have you been to visit mother's grave yet?" said Robin. "I went there this morning."

"No, I haven't," said Trevor. In fact he wondered whether he could find her tombstone for which he had engraved verses of his own composition.

Robin was silent. He too wished to say something, but couldn't find the words. It was easier to programme a computer than to talk to his father. Once when he had come home from university for a weekend, Trevor had offered him five pounds but he wouldn't take the money.

"No, thanks," he had said, "I have enough." Was it Trevor rather than Robin who had been selfish, doling out his emotions sparsely like a miser? Robin would never forgive him for his mother's death: that was clear to Trevor.

"We had to make sure that Frances is not bullied in school," he told Trevor.

"Oh?"

"Well, if you work at all in school nowadays the other pupils make a dead set at you. She's very scholarly and shy, if you see what I mean. She reads a lot. It worries me that she has so few friends."

"She doesn't?"

"Maybe we've kept her too secure, sheltered her too much. One can make a mistake that way too."

Trevor noted the last word, but didn't comment on it. Robin and his wife had built a shield of stainless steel around Frances: she was their prisoner. Maybe one could give too much love: or was it love? Robin was compensating for what had happened to himself: unto the third and fourth generation. . . . Perhaps he had made a fatal incorrigible mistake with Frances. Any time Trevor had seen her she struck him as remote, watchful.

"Does the woman still come to do the stair?" Robin asked.

"Yes, she's a true blue Tory. Very meticulous about the stairs.

Very anti-working-class. Too much violence everywhere, she says, but her favourite programme is *The Sweeney*. She doesn't want to be a servant."

"Does she bend down to wash them or does she use a squeegee?"

"I think she uses a squeegee." Julia probably had bent down. In his mind's eye he could see her scrubbing carefully. He closed his eyes against the sight.

"Had you not better buy a smaller flat?" Robin persisted.

"No." He didn't want to buy a flat somewhere else while the problem of the Camerons remained unsolved. It was like running away after his wife was dead. Perhaps he was a masochist. He wanted to suffer at least as much as she had. But anyway, he was prevented from leaving by the thought of the work of putting his books in cases, packing up curtains, moving the cooker.

"I see you've been painting," said Robin.

"Yes."

Sometimes when he stood on a chair or a stepladder to paint the ceiling he felt dizzy, as if he was about to fall. He trembled like a compass needle seeking true north. But he wasn't going to reveal his weakness to Robin.

"Well, I'll have to go," said Robin. He was leaving again and they hadn't really spoken to each other. They were still like Romans wearing their shields. He watched as Robin drove away.

Then he walked down town.

He would take a walk as far as the War Memorial which stood by the sea, a short distance from the centre of the town. Two soldiers were carved on it, one helping another through a field of stone. There was a water bottle slung at his side and a rifle in his hand. The sea stretched away from the War Memorial. Ships passed now and again, reflected in the water.

The town had changed since he had come to it. Shops had changed hands in a Darwinian struggle for survival. Since the

recession the buildings were tattier, lacking a coat of paint. He
used to have strange notions, such as that the town was like a
theatre, a back cloth for continuing drama. One day he would
see a young man pushing a pram, the next he was middle-aged
and stout. The same people were perpetually changing roles.
Oh, to be simple and see the world as it truly was! Once he
thought he saw Mrs Cooper standing with a message bag at
Liptons. He blinked but she was gone. The town seethed with
ghosts. At other times he felt that, as he was walking along, there
was a tall mirror in front of him.

He would go down to the quay and watch the boats. He
would see sitting on a deck a man sewing a green net with a
needle of bone. Orange buoys glowed. Seagulls stood on
bollards staring out to sea.

It was a beautiful town, in the summer especially, but best of
all he liked it in the autumn when the leaves were turning
golden. October was the best month of all. At times like these he
felt an elegiac sweetness in the air. The trees were surrendering
their crowns, abdicating. It was the month of Keats, the month
of the migrating birds. There was a touch of frost in the air: he
could feel it crackling on his teeth. Julia on the other hand had
preferred the spring: that was the difference between the Taurus
and the Capricorn.

There were tourists from all over the world. He passed an
Indian woman, delicate-boned and lovely; she reminded him of
London where there had been an Indian family in the same
tenement. He sat down on a bench and watched the sea.

A man wearing a white hat sat down beside him. It turned out
that he was from Chicago, unmarried, but he saved his money
for a trip abroad every year. He had been to Spain, New
Zealand, Japan. New Zealand was his favourite country.
During the winter he watched TV and read books, but never
drank. He saved his money for his foreign trips. He had found
the Londoners the most bad-mannered of all the people he had
met. Once he had been looking for a street and had asked a
flower seller where it was.

"It's not my business to give you directions," the flower seller had told him.

He stayed in lodgings and only had his pension. But he saved every penny. Curiously enough, Trevor quite liked the little man: he somewhat resembled Cooper. He hadn't allowed himself to vegetate. He had the innocent curiosity of the American. Trevor himself had seen little of the world. This man had walked on his own through the streets of Tokyo: talked confidently and knowledgeably about various currencies, passports, visas.

Trevor had noticed before that he was a target for lonely people. Beggars always came to beg from him. It was as if they sensed in him a vulnerability like their own. If there were six people on the one street he could guarantee that the beggar would come over to him. He gazed out at the water: the wind was blowing over it, composing shadows. An island stood out in the bay. A tall white ship was being loaded with cargo.

He rose and walked over to the station to see what magazines they had. There were two drunks there, singing, waving bottles. He bought a *Listener* and was leaving, when he saw Mrs Miller sitting on a bench, a bottle beside her. She noticed him and turned away. He made as if to speak to her and then decided against it. She wouldn't want to speak. Her fur coat was open and her face was swollen with drink. A train was about to depart. Poor woman, this was her solution to her problem. He looked at her as if looking at himself.

The two drunks had begun to quarrel with each other. One was swearing at the other one and waving his bottle like a weapon. A policeman strolled quietly and sedately towards them. Trevor left.

It is not natural for a man to be alone, he thought. When Julia was alive he didn't know what loneliness was. In fact in those days he wanted to be alone but he hadn't then understood what this void was like, how deep it went, how unreal it made the world. All that was meaningful became meaningless.

One of the drunks was struggling with the policeman who was talking into his walkie-talkie.

"F . . k off," the drunk shouted.

The policeman's arm was strong and steady on his.

The sun blazed on the water. An auctioneer was selling fish, boxes stacked around him. Some visitors were taking photographs. The white ship was beginning to move away. Minute by minute we create the world, minute by minute we make pictures, thought Trevor, we are artists of the universe.

The man from Chicago had left his seat. Trevor could see him in the distance entering a shop that sold tweeds. The shops hung out their webs to attract the flies. Everything preyed on everything else. The theatre produced its endless play.

When he had come to the town first he used to go for long walks along the cliffs, where jackdaws played with each other, diving and ascending. Boats' engines had hummed with a sound like bees, like pots on boil on a lazy Sunday.

A Chinaman stood outside his restaurant, inhaling the fresh air. Yellow man, yellow lamps, yellowness. He liked Chinese restaurants. They reminded him of churches; music leaked from their walls. Always there were ancient black telephones and dragons painted on the walls. He didn't like the food though he liked the building. Julia had liked Chinese food, Indian food; she was a true Taurus.

The Chinaman returned to his restaurant to continue his work. They worked like slaves, these people. They were perhaps from Hong Kong, not communists: on the contrary they believed in capitalism, who more? How did they like living in a country which was not their own? Exiles. He remembered reading in a paper recently of a North Vietnamese who had settled in Northern Ireland: he thought that the place was quiet and decent and pleasant. All was relative.

Maybe he should get out more. There was a chess club in the town. Perhaps he could attend it with his sleeping dozing friend. But he had never liked playing chess against people; he preferred solving problems: white to mate in two no matter what black did. That was another way in which he spent his Sundays.

Or again, he could join that committee about the oak tree. Or maybe he could phone Miss Gillespie who had hosted his poetry reading. He had liked her: she was quite like Julia.

Or . . .

He must make an opening into the world or he would end up like Mrs Floss, Mrs Miller. If he could not join the world, how could he call himself a poet? Milton had written, even though blind, Beethoven had composed, though deaf. After all he had his health and his faculties: he must make an effort. Why, he might even go to Cambridge to visit his computer son, take a pilgrimage to ask for forgiveness among the beautiful colleges becalmed in their world of knowledge, good and virtuous. Maybe he would like Cambridge. He felt restless somehow, as if the weather itself were demanding action from him. If he stayed day after day in the flat he would become useless, immobile. He might even lose the use of his legs. 'Poet loses legs after sitting in ivory tower composing lyrics.'

Self, self, self. The waves followed each other on to the shore, each perhaps separate, sufficient. The boats were selves, clear cut, definite. The auctioneer was a dramatist conscious of the admiration of the tourists. The world was a paean of selves; demanding to be heard, to be known. The stones lay on their shadows, impenetrable, austere. To break free from the self, to heal the wounded consciousness. To himself each ordinary man was as important as Beethoven. Even that stair-woman provided herself with an alibi as to why she had 'stooped' to what she was doing.

A policeman and a policewoman paced the pavement side by side, soberly, sedately. The drunk who had been taken away to jail was a self: his feelings cried out for mercy, audience. Selves bloomed at him from all directions. Even the seagulls pecking at old bones like dead crosswords had their shrieking crying selves. He steadied himself against stone, passing his hand across his brow. Even the tenement was a self, arising in stone from out of the undifferentiated nothingness. The worms nodding their heads were selves. Like the U-boats they seethed under the earth, under the stone, like a choir swaying to a baton.

Self, self, self. All those years he had justified his own self, leaving bloodstains and havoc behind him. He was responsible for his son turning into a computer, his wife dying. And for what? For a few poems that would soon be forgotten. Only genius could justify such inhumanity. If that.

Once he had seen Julia weeping at a film that she was watching on TV. "What's wrong?" he asked her.

"Nothing. Leave me alone." The film had been *Anna Karenina*. I could weep for Dido, Augustine had said. Not for my own soul, but for Dido. Such simple feelings. The only time he had ever wept was when Julia had died. That night he had asked himself, "What use my Dante now?" And of course Dante had been no use—in that blue raw morning with the birds beginning to sing.

Such simple feelings, and he had lost his. He had turned into a man of ice. He had built his shield and now it was melting. Better to weep than to be a man of ice. Better to shout, scream, than exist in silence. Better to strike out in passion than to be cold.

He was a comic, not a tragic man in his crushed hat. He saw himself limping along like a flawed anchorite. Poet as perpetual spy. Poet as spectator. Poet as metaphysical tramp. He imagined himself in a vast courtroom and a judge with a hearing aid bending down and saying, "What did you say, Life? Please explain?" (As if he were asking, who are the Beatles, the Rolling Stones. Judges were supposed not to know anything about the world outside the courtroom.)

"What is life?" this judge would ask, bending towards him. And he would say, "Life is . . . life is . . . life." But he couldn't define it further no matter how much the people in the courtroom rocked with laughter.

"Life is." And the audience slapped their sides. "Life is . . ." And the judge smiled, showing his false teeth. Everything about him false, his hearing aid, his teeth, his robe, his wig. They hid a skeleton. And a bird flew in through an open window. Life is life . . .

Linda and John were two years married. Linda had been a hairdresser before she married. John was working in a freezer shop and wanted to become an electrician, as his wages were small. He also had an ambition to own a TV repair shop one day. They had stayed in the middle flat for a while, then they had moved into the bottom flat when the matron died. They were, of course, the youngest couple in the tenement.

When John went to work in the morning Linda made herself a cup of coffee, but had stopped smoking since the baby was due shortly. She was radiant, happy. So was John who wanted a child too. Sometimes Linda felt sorry for the other people in the tenement: they were so old and so lonely most of them. She herself had never been lonely in her life: she came from a family of seven. Ever since she was eleven she wanted to be a hairdresser and had loved the job. It was clean and it was creative. It was also quite well paid. But when she became pregnant she decided that she would give up her job and John agreed. They would have less money, but it was important that the baby should have every chance. To bring up a child was what she wanted most in the world, what she had been born for. She was one of those women who are not greedy for possessions, her temperament was calm and tranquil.

One morning when she was drinking her coffee at about eleven o'clock, there was a knock on the door. She wondered at first whether it might be the milkman or the coalman, or the insurance man, but it was none of these. There was a tall gaunt man of about thirty-five standing on the doorstep: he wore rimless glasses. He stared at her and she stared back. There was something odd about the man, she felt immediately. It was as if he was staring through her, past her. She shivered slightly.

"What is it?" she asked.

He didn't answer. Then amazingly he said, "May I come in, please?"

His voice was dull, dead, without any expression in it.

"Are you selling something?" she said.

"No. May I come in?" Then before she could do anything to prevent him he had walked past her. Thinking about it afterwards, she couldn't understand quite how it had happened. It was as if somehow he slid past her without her noticing. She looked at Cooper's door, but remembered that he would be working in the toilets. She didn't know what to do. The man had not offered her any violence. He looked in fact pitiful, haggard. She followed him in. He was gazing round the lobby.

"The wallpaper's different," he said. "This wasn't here," and he pointed to the hall stand that she and John had bought at the market. It seemed to disturb him: he studied it for a long time.

She was so astonished that she didn't know what to say. He went into the bathroom and examined it. There were baby things already in the bathroom, for example a yellow duck that she had bought in Woolworth's. There were soaps, sponges, toothbrushes, shaving tubes, pink toilet paper. The bathroom suite was pink: the lampshade matched both it and the toilet paper. There were towels hung on silver rails. At a sale she had bought paper which she had placed on the window, and which gave an illusion of stained glass, so that the bathroom actually looked like a church, a shrine.

"And this is different, too," he said. "The bath we had was very big, white." He seemed stunned as if he had walked from one world into another one.

"Look," she said, "who are you?"

"Michael," he said.

"Michael who?" she said.

"Grant," he replied. "Michael Grant, I was passing," he said.

"Passing?"

"Yes, I was passing. I saw the window. There were different curtains. I wanted to see. Ours used to be green. Mother liked them green."

She was a little frightened now. Yet she must remain calm.

Not that he looked violent, in fact he looked quite dead, with his dead voice.

"I drove," he said. "I drove far. I left my car round the side."

He walked into the living room. "She used to sit there at the window," he said. "Knitting. She would watch the traffic."

He sat down on the sofa. "This was not red," he said. "This used to be yellow. And it used to face a different way." He shivered as if he were frightened. "I don't like it," he said.

"She used to watch the buses and the people. She never went out at the end. I remember that. I should have done more for her. Still, it couldn't be helped. She never liked Diana, you see."

"Diana?"

"She thought she was a money grabber and that she wasn't suitable. She was right."

"Is there something wrong?" said Linda. "I don't . . ." and then, inspired, "Would you like a cup of tea?" She didn't want to lose control, though this was a nightmare. She felt that she must step as if on glass, in a minefield. The man was dazed as if he had lost his memory. Now and again he passed his hand across his eyes.

"You've got an electric fire, too," he said. "There was a coal fire there once. I see you've closed it in. The coal was very dirty: every morning I used to bring a bucketful in. In the winter it was frosted over and I used a hammer to break it."

He stood up. "The church is the same. She used to watch the weddings and the funerals."

"Who did?" Linda said.

"Mother, of course."

"Oh."

There was silence. The man took out a cigarette case and picked a cigarette from it.

"Do you smoke?"

"No thanks."

"I used to have an ashtray on the arm of this sofa," he said. "And there was a little table and a sideboard. She kept her letters in the sideboard, her business letters."

Linda thought, "I should slip out and phone John. I wish I had a phone in the house, but we couldn't afford one."

But at the same time she wasn't frightened of the man, it was just that he was so strange, as if numb. Now and again he drew his coat collar around his neck as if he was cold, though it was a fine sunny day.

"You used to stay here?" she said.

"Yes. A long time ago. And then I married Diana. My mother didn't like her. 'You mark my words, that one will leave when she's had enough', she used to tell me." He lit his cigarette with a trembling hand. "Maybe I could see the bedroom," he said. Without asking her permission he walked down the lobby and opened the door of the bedroom. This had a blue motif. There was a blue counterpane on the bed and a blue lampshade.

"It's the wrong way round," he said. "I used to have my radio there. I used to listen to it a lot. I had my books over there. In that corner. I could hear mother working in the kitchen. She used to listen to the Silver Lining; a religious programme." He picked up the rabbit which she had bought in advance for the child, and looked at it for a long time before putting it down again.

Then he left the room. She followed him as if it was she who was the stranger, and not him. She wondered what would happen if John came in. He would throw this man out, he would be very angry, he would be thinking that she was having an affair. He had such a temper when he was roused.

"I'm just going out," she said hopefully. "I do my shopping about now."

"I'll wait till you come back if you like," he said dully.

"But I can't leave you here on your own," she said.

"Why not?"

"Why not? I can't. That's all. My husband will be coming in shortly. He comes home for a coffee."

"Oh."

He sat down on the sofa again.

"She warned me about Diana. We were married for four

years, four years yesterday. Yesterday, she left. She left a note. I drove up here. Mother said I should never have married her. 'She'll run away, you mark my words', she said. She was right. She wanted everything she could get. Behind my back she was running up bills with expensive shops. You can go, I told her, but I didn't think she would choose that day. Then I took the car and I drove. I don't know why I am here." And he passed his hand across his brow.

"This man has escaped from somewhere," thought Linda. "He's a madman." But he hardly seemed to notice that she was there or if he did he thought of her as an interloper. What could she do? She couldn't even push him out. She couldn't leave him in the house. John wouldn't be back till one o'clock. Cooper wasn't in. Mrs Floss would probably be in bed. And Trevor Porter might be typing.

"When was it you lived here?" she asked.

"Twenty years ago. About that." His eye moved away from her to the space at the window, which had once held the chair on which his mother used to sit. "Then we left. Four years ago I married Diana. I worked in a library. She didn't think my pay was high enough. Not enough money, she said."

"And what's your name again?"

"Michael Grant."

"And you stayed in this flat?"

"Yes. But it was different then. There was a different name on the door. I looked at your window for a long time. I thought to myself, 'Who stays there now?' I used to get very tired and my mother would tell me to stay in bed. She didn't want me to marry Diana. Diana was beautiful. I met her in the other place, in the other town." He tried to remember the name but couldn't.

"She and my mother didn't get on. She gave me an ultimatum. Your mother will have to go or I go. And mother went. To a Home. I used to visit her. Look what you've done to me, she would say. But Diana said that she couldn't stay in the same house as her. She said my mother was an evil woman and made up stories about her. She said my mother would leave the electricity on to make things more expensive. She was very difficult, Diana said. She thought everything she said was right. She said my mother hated her. I could see it wouldn't work and so she had to go to the Home. Diana wouldn't go to visit her. But I did. Every Sunday I went. When am I getting home, my mother would say, when are you getting rid of that evil woman? But I couldn't get rid of her: Diana was very strong willed. She would go into rages and throw things. She would have fits if she didn't have her own way. In the end it was easier to give into her, I found that. I didn't stand up to her. 'You must stand up to her', my mother would say. 'She's a bad, bad woman'. 'It's her or me', Diana would say."

"I'm sorry," said Linda.

"She left me yesterday. There was a note under the door when I got home from my work. She said I should have married my mother. You're her child. Her baby." Linda shivered. The baby jumped in her womb.

"You don't know what it was like. I was between the two of them for four years. And then my mother died in the Home. 'You'll live to regret this', she told me. 'These are my last words to you'. 'Good riddance', that's what Diana said. She called her an old bag."

He stared down at the floor. "Are you sure you won't take a cup of tea," said Linda.

"No, thank you. I don't like tea."

"We stayed here," he said. "I'm sure there's none of the people left now whom we knew. The door is still the same colour. I noticed that. We always wanted to paint the door, but no one would agree on the colour. One wanted one colour and someone else another. I would have paid for it, though I didn't have much money. There was a painter here and he would have painted it but no one would decide on a colour. So nothing was done. I remember there were old bells hanging there from the ceiling. When you pulled the bell outside, the bells in here would tinkle. There was also an old range which we gutted. The flat cost two thousand pounds, it was in such bad condition. From the moment that we got married Diana wanted a washing machine. Mother never had a washing machine: she hung the clothes out on the line. Usually on Monday mornings." He took out a handkerchief and wiped his face with it. His face sweated palely.

"My name's Linda, and my husband's name is John. We're called Mason," she said.

"Oh. I should like to sleep."

"You can't sleep here," she said. "John will be coming in shortly for his coffee. I told you."

"Coffee?" And then, "I don't know you."

"Did you come by car?" she said.

"Yes, I left it round the corner. There was a big lorry. I hope it will be safe. There's much more traffic here now and more yellow lines. It was only after I got married that I bought a car. Second hand. Diana said everybody has a car nowadays. My mother used to ask me to buy a car so she could go for runs, because she was tired staring out of the window. But I didn't buy one. I was nervous in those days. Diana made me buy one, and I learnt to drive. I left early this morning and drove here. There was a very slow car in front of me. It was driven by an old man in a bowler hat."

Linda looked around her. Suddenly she saw a big black range instead of her electric fire. Then she saw a chair at the window. An old woman was sitting on it knitting. For some reason she fancied she saw a Bible beside her. She felt disorientated. It was odd; she had never felt like this before. Mr Cooper might be coming home shortly. Sometimes, not every day, he would come home for his lunch. She would have been glad to see him, though John didn't like him. She would have preferred him to this ghost, this phantom, who wandered around like a lost soul. And her house suddenly became unreal. She must get a grip on herself. She must say to herself, this is my house, this is John's house, this is our house. Then it occurred to her, maybe this is a ghost. Maybe this isn't really happening, maybe I'm imagining it. Pregnant women often have odd notions. And she sweated suddenly. But he was there, he was definitely there, or was he? Of course he was. If she put her hand out she would be able to touch him. The tenement was, however, strangely silent. Not even the tapping of Trevor Porter's typewriter could be heard. It was as if she had stepped into a vacuum. And in the vacuum was herself and this thin man.

But she had never heard of anyone called Grant before. Cooper would know if there had been someone with that name. Mrs Floss wouldn't know: neither would Mr Porter. Mrs Miller, however, would know. She would leave the door open in case she happened to descend the stairs. She would be glad to see even her.

But then the man had said, 'Diana'. Could she have imagined that too? Of course not. The man was real, she was real. The house was real. He was sitting on the sofa again staring ahead of him. He was twisting his hat in his hand. Stay, she thought, you must stay till I can find someone else who will see you. But there was no one else. She could hear no movement in the flat. She could hear the silence.

"Diana didn't like the hospital," he said. "She was tall and fair. She was beautiful. I never knew why she married me. She deceived me. At first I thought everything would be all right. We used to go every Friday night to this particular hotel. I used to argue with her because she would smile at other men. She said that I was jealous and jealousy was bad. But she did smile at other men. Pull your skirt down, I would whisper to her. But she wouldn't. 'I like that man, he's handsome', she would say. The quarrels we had. I would apologize: it was always me who apologized, and I would leave flowers for her. But I was going through hell just the same. If only she would leave, I told myself, I would have peace. Last night I didn't sleep at all. I wanted to leave the house and drive somewhere, anywhere. And now I'm here. Why did I come here?" He stared at her blankly.

"Perhaps you were happy here."

"Maybe. I don't think I was, but maybe I was. I thought to myself, if my mother dies, I will marry. So I married anyway,

even before she died. She didn't like that. 'You betrayed me',
she would say. 'Look at all I've done for you and you betray me,
you put me in a Home. You wait', she said, 'she'll start finding
fault with me. That will be the first thing. I know women, you
don't. Your mother's not a fool. She's an old dog on a hard road.
You wait.'

"My mother was difficult right enough: she had ways of being
difficult. About the garden, for instance, and about the food. 'I
never used to make food like this', she would say. Diana liked
Chinese dishes, you understand. My mother liked simple food,
mince, tripe, things like that. She wouldn't eat the food Diana
cooked. 'She's always putting sauce on everything', she would
complain. 'I can't stand it. When can we have some proper
food?'

"But I didn't want to offend Diana. No, she wasn't like you.
She was tall and blonde. She never visited mother in the Home.
I used to go and see her. It broke my heart. 'It was you who put
me here', she would say. 'If you had stood up to Diana. But you
never would'." His eyes fastened themselves on Linda. "I never
stood up to anyone."

Please let someone come, thought Linda. Even my father-in-
law. He's real, he may be a drunkard but he's real. But there was
no sound everywhere, she might as well have been on a desert.

"Listen," she said suddenly, "will you do something for me?
Can I take your photograph?"

"My photograph? What for?"

"I want to show it to my husband when he comes."

"If you like. What does it matter." She went into the bedroom
and found the camera. She set it quickly and took his
photograph sitting on the sofa. He didn't smile. His face was
fixed, stony. "That's done," she said. "Thank you. And now I
really must go. I have to get the messages." And she made for the
door. But he didn't follow her. He still sat where he was.

"I remember," he said, "the little boys would scramble for
pennies outside the church. The bride would throw them out of
the car when she was leaving. Diana wanted to be married in a

registry office. 'Why should we spend money on a church wedding', she said, 'when we could buy a car with it?' But mother said, 'What nonsense. Of course you'll have a church wedding. Greed', she said, 'nothing but greed. You won't feel properly married in a registry office'."

Linda herself had been married in white. She thought her heart would break with happiness. She was frightened and nervous and was ten minutes late arriving at the church on her father's arm. When she answered the minister her voice was very low, so that people could hardly hear her. But she danced all night at the reception, and then they left to go on their honeymoon. John was handsome, assured, he knew everything. The way he talked to the manager of the hotel! Where had he learnt to do that? She had never been out of her home town in her whole life.

The man wandered over to the window. "You've changed them," he said. "When I was here you had to pull on a rope. It was very complicated. The window opened out like a door. Mother used to clean them. Sometimes I would clean them too. I remember the spring when we used to clean them. The days were so breezy and everything sparkled." His pain-filled eyes regarded her from a gaunt face: he was unshaven. He looked as if he hadn't slept for days. Now and again he would put his hand to his breast pocket as if checking that his wallet was there.

"What happened to Diana?" said Linda.

"I don't know, maybe she ran away with someone. She took some of the money that I had in a drawer. She left an IOU but I'll never see the money again. I know that."

Suddenly Linda felt sick. She rushed into the bathroom, pulled the door behind her and threw up. Bent over, she stared into the lavatory bowl. She clutched the side of the bath and spewed, kneeling on the floor in front of the mock stained-glass window. Finally she staggered to her feet and gazed into the mirror. Her face was very white. Oh God, she thought, I must run out of here, I must go for help. I mustn't lose my baby, whatever happens. She thought, I can leave him in the house, he's like a zombie, he won't do any harm. On the other hand, he might lock herself and John out. He was mad, not violently mad, but queer. His eyes were funny, she had never seen eyes like that before. They were perfectly dead as if they had seen all there was to see and had finally turned away from the world.

She wiped her mouth on the towel. And she leaned against the door for a moment. She had responsibility to her child. It was hers and also John's. She must think what was best. She was frightened; of that there was no doubt. She would make a dash for the door. She opened the bathroom quietly. She ran for the front door and then for some reason looked back. The living room was empty. She walked back into the room. There was no one there. It was perfectly blank. She flinched and then she ran out of the house as if chasing her vision: he must just have gone. He had said he had left his car at the side of the tenement behind a lorry. She passed a big lorry parked below the side window. But there was no car behind it. She asked the lorry driver if he had seen a car driving out.

"No," he said.

"Did you see a car pull in about half an hour ago?" she said.

"No," he said, looking at her queerly.

"A friend of mine," she said. "I was expecting her but she hasn't come."

She walked back to the flat. The house was empty, quiet. The sofa showed no imprint of anyone's body. The sun shone in through the window. Her heart began to slow down. She sat on the sofa. She tried to think. Of course there was the photograph she had taken. The camera was lying on a chair opposite the sofa. She would take the spool down to the chemist's when she did her shopping.

She and John must leave this place, she didn't like it. They must try and get a council house, a new house, one that hadn't been lived in before.

"You're not like Diana," the voice had said. Of course she knew that. She looked in the mirror for a long while. Then she made herself a cup of coffee. The cup trembled in her hand. The walls of the house seemed to be moving in and out like plasticine. The coffee, however, helped her. Of course he had been there. He had left when she had gone to the bathroom, it was as simple as that. He didn't look the type who would drive a car: about that he had been fantasizing. And of course he probably wasn't married at all. That too was fantasy. What tall, golden haired woman would marry a man like him? His story was a web of lies, a rigmarole. How could she have been taken in by it. And then again, she would find out if there had been a Grant here in the past. He would have come by bus, or perhaps by train. He would have seen the flat from the top window of a bus.

I must get out of here, she thought. I must go for the messages. I must talk to someone. The typewriter was now tapping. She could hear it quite clearly like a woodpecker. Funny she hadn't heard it before. What a poor life that man had, what a dreadful life. Between his mother and Diana. Suddenly she had a terrible thought. She went into the bathroom. There was a *Daily Record* lying on the side of the bath where John had left it that morning. There was a headline. It said, 'Diana expecting her second child'. She stared at it for a long time. No, it wasn't false, he had been there. The photograph would show that. And surely, he hadn't made up all that stuff about his mother. And he had said 'Grant'. She could remember that quite clearly. She took out her straw message bag, shut the door behind her, and set off to the Co-op. 'Savings on beans', it said in the window. She walked in. There was a young girl with a gun pasting prices on tins. She smiled at her and the girl smiled back. The manager was standing at the far end of the shop watching what was going on.

"Morning, Mrs Mason," he said.

"Good morning," she said.

Music was playing gently. She bent down to take two pints of milk. She must also remember the cereal. She pushed the trolley ahead of her like a pram. The baby stirred in her belly. She placed the pints of milk in the trolley and wheeled it forward.

The ashtray, she thought. He smoked a cigarette. I remember

that. She left the trolley where it was. She walked briskly out of the shop. Her heels clicked on the pavement as she hurried back to the flat. He had definitely smoked. There was ash on the tray: she could remember seeing it. There must be.

HUGH CAMERON WAS a big heavy man. In previous years he had been a long-distance lorry driver: now however he was a labourer. He had, in fact, been sacked as a long-distance lorry driver because of his heavy drinking. He still drank heavily, and much more aggressively. His aggression which ate him up couldn't be contained for long. He often thought that if he had had a family this aggression would not be simmering so persistently inside him. There had been times when he had been taunted by his workmates with being impotent till they had learned the viciousness of his temper.

When he was a long-distance lorry driver he had had enough casual sex from students, for example, thumbing lifts, and it was understood that they would pay in the only currency they had. If sex was not freely forthcoming, then he would threaten physical violence. Thus he compensated for his wife's fastidiousness, as he had done when serving in France during the war. He remembered those days with nostalgia; when there was terror, destruction, elation everywhere, and cigarettes could buy whatever one wanted. A good man could survive among those ruins, that wilderness.

He had actually been brought up by a stepfather, his mother having married twice. He hated his stepfather, thought him a scholastic poof. One day he had hit him and knocked him down. Then he had walked out of the house. His stepfather had said he must not communicate with them again. He had actually threatened to burn down the house, but his stepfather said that he would have no hesitation in calling the police. At that time he drank heavily. He thought himself unloved, unwanted. He felt that his stepfather had influenced his mother against him. Twice he was picked up by the police for brawling, once at a football match and once in a pub when he was demanding drink after hours.

He was a fanatical Rangers' supporter, had worn the honourable blue scarf and carried the blue banner. He thought Catholics, Fenians, were the scum of the earth: they should not be allowed to live. At a Rangers-Hibernian match he had tried to jump on the bonnet of a car of a Hibs supporter, banging on the windscreen. The police had picked him up and bundled him into the van, where he had fought ferociously till he had been punched in the stomach and sat on.

"Would you say this gentleman was a Catholic?" one of the policemen said in the posh Edinburgh voice.

"I would say that," said the other policeman. "Next thing you know he'll be complaining about police brutality." They stripped him down in the station and threw him into a cell where he sang Rangers' songs.

"Not a nice voice," said the first policeman, who wore spectacles.

"Not classical," said the other one sadly.

He was fined fifty pounds. After that he hated policemen. In spite of the fact that he supported the Queen, he didn't like the law, which was a paradox that he didn't investigate.

The second time he was picked up he was demanding drink in a pub after he had lost his job as a long-distance lorry driver. Again he had been stripped and thrown into a cell. He called the policemen fat pigs: he shivered in his cell, but still continued to sing.

He was fifty-nine years old, but still strong physically. When drunk he sang hymns but with words like 'Hang the Pope on an Orange Rope'. He had always wanted to go to Northern Ireland, but had never been. One day, however, he would go there. He talked a great deal about King William and the Boyne and the Derry boys. He imagined himself as a hero on a white horse.

The aggression simmered and seethed inside him. He knew that he had made a mess of his life. Working as a labourer on the roads was not an achievement for any man. He believed that his wife was to blame for what had happened to him: she was always so pale, so insignificant, and she would never go to the pub with him. Once she had thought of saving up for a boarding house, but he didn't want that. In any case they didn't have the capital unless they borrowed it. Working with his spade on a frosty autumn day he would look around him at the leaves, which were losing their lustre, and feel unaccountably sad. He also thought that he was not quite as strong as he had been, though he did exercises. How long could one last as a labourer? And there was no possibility of any other job. He watched the beautiful cars speeding past and envied their drivers. He wished that he was still driving a long-distance lorry through the night. It had given him a sense of power with its hugeness. He could manoeuvre a very large lorry within a very tiny area.

Friday and Saturday nights, he was usually drunk. When he came home at night he couldn't stand the sight of his wife who looked so vulnerable and frightened. No matter how much and how often he beat her up she wouldn't send for the police. Another thing he liked was tormenting Porter, who reminded him of his stepfather: he had the same cool distant remote look as if he thought you were dirt. He would deliberately stamp on the ceiling with his heavy boots, shift wardrobes and sideboards about.

His wife sat and waited for him to come in drunk. His aggression was an uncontrollable force. It ate into him, devoured him. There was hardly any moment when it would leave him alone. Nor could he explain this aggression to anyone else. It arose from his powerlessness in the world. His force, therefore, was directed against his wife: it was the only power he had. And her very vulnerability, her very pallor, was an invitation for him to hit her. Sometimes he thought that she enjoyed being hit. He savoured the idea that the police could do nothing about his violence unless she charged him. He remembered those nights of late driving, anticipating what would happen later. Such sweet young flesh. Now there was none of that. His wife had complained of his absences from home in those days: and he blamed her for the loss of his job. If she had left him alone he would not have become drunk so often: he hated anyone trying to run his life.

He had married her when they were both twenty-four. This was at the time he had left his stepfather's house: he had met her at a dance. She came from a village about a hundred miles to the north, and had been brought up in a religious home. It was this martyred air about her that annoyed him more than anything else, her long suffering. She was afraid that if she sent for the police people would talk about her, and this in spite of the fact that they were doing so anyway, since she ran out screaming into the road at weekends, and she had black eyes continually, for whose existence she invented the most ingenious reasons. He wanted to laugh at the police, to show them that he wasn't afraid of them, but they left him alone, they wouldn't allow him that satisfaction. No matter how much she feared him, she didn't want to see him in prison.

Sometimes he thought, when he was hitting her, that it was his mother he was hitting. She had married a stepfather whom he hated; and had surrendered to his cold loveless nature. It was he who would say to her, "That boy is a lout, he has no sense of gentleness, tenderness: he is completely selfish, he won't wash any dishes, he comes in at night drunk, he sings his barbaric songs and tells his barbaric jokes."

By becoming a Rangers' supporter, he had been in fact searching for love, security. Among these people he had felt at home, felt wanted. His blue scarf was a badge of togetherness. He had an aim in life, to drive his team towards victory: it would be a victory of his own by proxy. He sometimes imagined that he was back in the army wearing a uniform. But his stepfather hadn't been interested in football: he had never played games in his life. He imagined him as cowering, bespectacled, in a toilet while the other boys were playing football: a winner of prizes, a poof. There was a complete and total lack of communication between the two of them. His stepfather didn't drink.

But it was his mother whom he hated more than his stepfather. After her first husband's death she shouldn't have married at all, or she should have married a Rangers' supporter. His stepfather wouldn't speak to him at meals. His silences were oppressive and cold: he had made the house glacial. He had read the *Guardian*, talked a lot of crap about crime and criminals. Anyone listening to him would have thought that he was caring, loving, whereas he was the very opposite of that. He had thought his stepson loutish, a being from outer space. His stepson compensated by behaving worse than he might otherwise have done. He became the blue-clad alien that his father despised.

His twin hates were Catholics and his wife. "What do you know about the Boyne?" his stepfather would say to him. "Who was the English King whom William deposed?" And he didn't know: he thought it was Henry the Eighth. His stepfather smiled his thin knife-like smile. Another triumph for him. But what did it matter if he didn't know what King it was? He knew that he hated the Catholics, Fenian bastards. His colour was Orange: Derry's wall would protect him. His happiest times were at football matches.

It was amazing that Greta had married him. But she too had come from a family that didn't like Catholics. She belonged to the Free Church: naturally she didn't drink or smoke. Catholics thought that by breeding furiously they would inherit the world. Maybe she should have bred freely too. But he couldn't stand the fact that while the Catholics were breeding secretly and victoriously, he wasn't. One should be doing one's bit to keep these bastards in their places.

In fact he sometimes thought she looked like a Catholic herself, like the Virgin Mary. She was so pale, so white, like a plaster saint. She was long-suffering, patient.

During the week he could be friendly, companionable. He had a number of jokes about the Catholics that he told her. Some however, were very sick and she didn't like them. He had even been known to make the dinner when he was in a good mood. But he would never wash or dry dishes. That was for women to do. Even when she was sick, disabled, he would never wash a dish.

But no matter what he did, the aggressiveness never wholly left him. He thought that people in the town despised him. Only Mrs Miller would speak to him. Porter would pass him on the stair without even glancing at him. Yet on Saturday mornings Hugh would dress up neatly, was bright and happy, as he set out for the pub. Why, he had been known to say "Good morning" to Trevor, though never to Mason. Mason was a Catholic bastard, beginning the process of breeding. All these Catholics went to the same butcher, the same grocer, stuck together. They were a secret society. On Saturday mornings he looked handsome in his blue suit, shaved closely but never used shaving lotion: shaving lotion was for poofs. The world seemed to him free and open on Saturday mornings. He was good-humoured, pleasant.

But as the day wore on, as he drank more and more, the devil began to possess him, the aggression simmered and boiled. Sometimes he would meet Mrs Miller at the station and they would sing a song together. Now there was a woman for you. She had the right ideas too, didn't like the blacks or the Catholics.

When he climbed the stairs on Friday or Saturday nights he staggered from side to side. There was silence everywhere. He often thought that he should bang on Porter's door or ring the doorbell and, when he came out, punch him in the face, he reminded him so much of his stepfather. But Porter was curiously quiet: he never met him on a Friday or Saturday night, though he might meet Mrs Porter who had once talked to him seriously about his wife. At least she had guts. She was tougher than her husband, she had once organized them against the landlord and won a respite from roof repairs. He admired her, but disliked her husband.

When he came home he would ask for his dinner and would eat it broodingly as the aggression built up inside him. His wife sat at the table watching him. He hated people watching him. Why didn't they turn their eyes away? Sometimes she sighed heavily. Sometimes she was so nervous that she would drop a cup or a plate. If this happened he would become even more aggressive than before. He might smash some plates to match hers, She was so patient, he couldn't finally break her. He could make her run screaming into the roadway, but he couldn't break her. She would shout for help, but no one would come. Not the neighbours certainly. Once a tall fellow, a visitor to the town, who had been walking past at the time in the twilight, had tried to interfere but he had made short work of him. It was none of his business.

After he had beaten her up he would hear her weeping as she lay in bed. And her weeping irritated him even more than her silence. "Shut up," he would shout, "shut up, shut your bloody mouth." But she would still carry on weeping though she would try to stuff a handkerchief in her mouth. She didn't have to go out labouring as he had to. She was too futile to earn money. If he drank, wasn't it his own money he was using? She had never earned a penny in her life.

And yet in spite of everything, she was up on Sunday morning cooking his bacon and eggs. The house was quiet then, rested, as after a storm. You could hear yourself breathe, he could be tender to her, sometimes even remorseful. Could she not understand that he couldn't help himself? Sometimes he even made good resolutions; he would work, he would have a future. But by the end of the week, following chaste virginal Sunday, the aggression had built up in him again.

She had once left him to go to her father's house, but she had come back of her own free will. Why was that? He couldn't understand it. The house was a mess when she returned, and she cleared dirty dishes away in silence. Her father, of course, had told her time and time again to leave her husband and to come and stay with him, but she didn't want to. She was frightened of what the villagers would say about her, that she couldn't keep her man, that her marriage had failed. And in any case, she didn't have any money and her father only had his pension. And it was so quiet where he lived. It was extraordinary, almost as if she missed the noise, the din. She had loved her husband in the past, sometimes even loved him now when he was in a good humour: he could be quite charming. She could laugh at his jokes, but at other times she told him that he ought to see a psychiatrist. But of course he never would. Imagine a Rangers' supporter going to see a psychiatrist! He wasn't a poof like that. No, she didn't miss the beatings: on the contrary, she dreaded them. She missed the good qualities that were buried inside him, what he could be on a good day. He should go to church, even though he was a rabid Protestant.

"How can you hate the Catholics so much?" she would say to him. (Her Free Church friends, some of them, didn't like the Catholics, but she herself didn't mind them.) "They go to the church. You don't. They get up early in the morning to go to mass, they give a lot of money to their church." But he didn't see any contradiction in that. No, not at all. She could see it, however, and in fact she liked Linda and John. They were in love with each other, she had given them presents in preparation for the coming of the baby. Linda would sometimes invite her in for a coffee and be tactful about her black eyes. No, she wouldn't tell Linda about her husband. Yet sometimes she almost wept when she saw Linda and John together. They were so happy, their child was about to be born.

The tenement would be renewed. At the moment there were only old people, single people, those who had no future. At least John and Linda had a future. And like the other young ones they would move into a council house when the flat became too small for their growing family.

She had often apologized to Mrs Porter. "I'm sorry," she would say. And Mrs Porter would make a distinction between herself and her husband; "Why don't you tell him to leave?" she would say.

"It's his flat."

"Why don't you run away then? I would run away." But then Mrs Porter was a clever woman: she had been a secretary in a school.

"You could get a job," she would say to her. "One of these nights he'll kill you. Is there no organization you could consult? There must be an organization who would help someone like you."

"No, thanks," she would say.

Mrs Porter's house was always tidy, quiet. From one of the rooms she could hear the sound of a typewriter: Mr Porter never came in to see the two of them. He was much more remorseless than his wife: he didn't understand, didn't try to understand. Yet what could she do about it? Mrs Porter, on the other hand was a good woman. She helped that old man, and she was always putting flowers in the church. Mrs Porter would say to her, "Why don't you come to church with me?" But she wouldn't go, in case Hugh knew of it.

She was so bitterly ashamed. If she left her husband then Mr and Mrs Porter might have an easier life of it, for she knew that the former irritated her husband. But where could she go? She partly blamed herself for what had happened to Hugh. Maybe if she had been a better wife. He needed a lot of sex and she couldn't provide it. Her background was to blame for that. Her father had brought her up to think sex dirty and dangerous. Of course she knew that he had had other women, young girls, when he was a long-distance lorry driver. In fact he had boasted of it.

Christmas and New Year were the worst: she dreaded these. He would be drunk all the time as if there were a sanction for it at that season of the year. They had few friends, and he would never go first footing, the dark handsome stranger, but would sit sullenly drinking all through the holidays. While Christmas was for others the birth of the Child, he thought that Christmas was a drunken festival. The birth of the Child was associated in his mind with the Virgin Mary. He never sent Christmas cards and for a different reason she never sent any either: for her church believed that Christmas Day was not the true date of the Saviour's birth. He hated stained glass windows: he didn't like seeing pictures of Christ against a green background of the common earth. And then again New Year was even worse. While the New Year was for others the beginning of a new world, a fresh start, it was for her an exaggerated continuation of the old world. He was at his worst during Hogmanay. She wondered how at times like these the Porters put up with him. But Mrs Porter had told her that her husband was tired of moving.

She didn't dislike the tenement itself. They had moved in after the death of Mrs Brown. They had heard stories of her and the matron, how they were always tidying the close like witches with brooms. Hugh didn't give a damn about papers or bins: his own bin was full of empty whisky bottles. Sometimes she herself would wrap the bottles in paper so that the bin men wouldn't know whether they were lemonade bottles unless they unwrapped them. He wouldn't go to the shed for coal: she had to bring it up in buckets. The only paper he read was the Daily Record: he would sit for hours gazing at page three, which always had a naked woman on it.

She had never thought that her life would turn out the way it had done. When she was young she believed in romance, in willing bondage. She would look at the brides and bridegrooms outside the church and weep. "You watch," said Hugh, "you can always tell the f. . .ing Fenians. They bow when they go into the cathedral. And they can't understand what the priest says, he talks in Latin. And they make their confessions. They tell the priest, I was feeling up a nun, Father. It was at a disco." He never seemed to see that he himself was much worse than any of them, brutal, vicious, barbaric. She had never seen a Catholic as bad as him. It was funny to hear him attacking the Catholics for being beasts while his own face was twisted with hate and he staggered about the kitchen.

One night he had scrawled on Mason's door, "Go home, you Fenian Bastard." She had seen John looking at it in the morning. He couldn't make up his mind who had done it, it might have been someone passing on the street late at night, since his flat was on the ground floor. Perhaps he had a shrewd idea that it was her husband. She couldn't be sure: but she didn't like the look he gave her. They said that he had a terrible temper when he was roused.

"That'll teach the bugger," Hugh laughed.

"I should watch him if I were you," she said in a quiet voice.

"Who, that Catholic bastard?" But he was growing fat, gross, he did too much sitting about.

One night he put his hand through the window on the stair and came in with blood pouring from it. Perhaps he was thinking of the Red Hand of Ulster. Perhaps he had imagined pictures on the window. "That's the blood of a good Proddy," he told her. "Proddy blood, that is. Fenian blood is green."

Another time he had beaten her up because she had bought a green tablecloth, which she had liked very much. In fact the ironic thing was that her favourite colour was green, but he made sure that the main colours in the flat were blue: blue wallpaper, blue linoleum. He wanted to paint the door in the close blue, and would have done so too, except that he was too lazy. She would have hated a blue door. He told her that a Rangers' supporter he had heard of refused to mow the lawn because it was green. None of her clothes were green. She even had to throw out one of her best hats and a handbag.

He wouldn't buy anything from the cafe near them because the owner was an Italian, and this in spite of the fact that the cafe was open late at night, long after the other shops had shut. "He puts up his prices, the Fenian bastard," he would say. "It was the same during the war. These Eyeties had no guts." He had served in the African desert and remembered those nights with nostalgia, millions of stars in the sky at night, camels, brothels. Sometimes he talked of becoming a mercenary and going to Africa or Arabia.

"These bloody blacks," he would say, "I would castrate the lot of them. They're as bad as the Fenians."

He loved hearing of Catholic missionaries, nuns, priests, being killed, and he was glad when Kennedy was assassinated. "Serve the f. . .ing Fenian right." He would look at the film over and over. "Wait for it, wait for it, you Fenian bastard!" he would shout, "Good old Oswald. A real Proddy."

He believed that nuns and priests slept with each other in convents and monasteries, and that their progeny was sent to South America. "That's the slave trade," he would say. "These nuns are hot stuff."

When he was drunk he sang anti-Catholic songs all the time. His jokes were sick. "What jumps up and down and falls apart," he would ask. The answer: "A leper on a trampoline." Or, "What is the picture of innocence? A nun who thought a French letter was a worm's bed."

He remembered the days he would call his stepfather, very formally, Mr Williamson. "How is Mr Williamson today?" he would ask his mother while his stepfather stared at him with fixed hopeless fury. "Does Mr Williamson want the milk?"

He would never tell his wife this, but sometimes when he was alone, he would burst into tears for no reason, especially when he was drunk. And he would beat his head against the table as if he liked the pain. Like that time he had thrust his fist through the window and the red had been like a burning bush. It would have been better if the blood had been blue. Passers-by had been blamed for the broken window too: it had been repaired eventually by Mrs Floss out of her own pocket. Stupid woman.

The only person in the close he had any respect for was Mrs Miller. She went her own way and didn't care what people thought of her. Often she would refuse to pay her rent. She stood out there in the open. She was quite right not to let anyone into her flat. They said that she had been pretty once, though she was pretty haggard now. A true Proddy if there ever was one. "You should go to Rhodesia," she had told him. "Put these guerillas down. You would like the life there." But even if he had wanted to, his wife wouldn't have gone. And anyway you had to have a trade. You had to have a trade to get into any of these countries. Australia even, he had thought of Australia, but the same was true for that country. There was an Australian artist in the town and one night in the pub he had said he would swallow anyone's sock. "You give me one of your socks," he had said to one of the lads, "and I'll swallow it." And he had, too, though he was sick after it. Then he had picked up an ashtray and gone round the pub with it: "You put your dandruff in that," he had said. He was a funny man. If more people were like that, life would be much happier for everybody. Though not all Australians were like that artist. One of them he had met in a pub had drunk his beer quietly, and looked like his stepfather.

He himself would sometimes dance on the tables and sing anti-I.R.A. songs. He had been put out of a few pubs for that. There was only the one pub in the town that he could go to now. Maybe eventually he wouldn't be able to go to any of them, and he would have to drink at home. To hell with them, he was one of the few honest people in the town.

"I loved my husband," Mrs Brown was supposed to have said. Imagine that. Silly old git, going to the cemetery every Sunday. And in a taxi too. "We were so happy," she used to say, apparently. But that was her story. Perhaps they hadn't been happy at all. Others said that she and her husband had quarrelled a lot. They owned a shop and he did all the paper work. After his death, she was lost. Nothing but death in this bloody tenement anyway. If only there were young people, girls preferably. Still it was better than some tenements he had seen.

Sometimes as Greta lay beside him in bed he would stare at her in amazement. How had he ever married her? She was like a statue. She had no life in her. He must have been mad. And yet that time she had been with her father for a fortnight, he had phoned her and even sent her flowers. He had sworn he would change if she came back. And she believed him too, and he had changed, for a month. But it hadn't lasted. The aggression inside him built up again. "I can't believe anything you say," she would say to him. "Nothing." But he needed help. Some being inside him was shouting out to her, "But can't you see that I need help. It isn't my fault. I'm dying of this aggression, this hatred. If I could help myself, do you think I would be acting like this?" And the moon shone down on her bloodless face with the black eye. It was as if she had been drained by a vampire. Somewhere there was a vampire eating them all up. It had green wings. It was a conspiracy of the Fenians; they were the enemy. They sucked the blood of Protestants.

One night he had been coming home down an empty street. There was a red kiosk and a yellow light shining on the road, like sickness. Oh, God, how he hated that yellow light, the colour of his stepfather's skin. It was as if he was walking through hell, through perpetual sickness. The post office was yellow in the light. He heard the din of his own footsteps. It was as if he was a picture made of cardboard. The kiosk was beaded with rain. The telephone cord hung down. There were wet newspapers on the floor. If he picked up the phone who would he be connected with? He stretched his hand out. It was shaking. His whole body was shaking. Little men jumped out of the telephone box. They were burning him. They were staring at him with scholastic eyes, quizzing him about the history of Ireland. Hundreds of little men. He shivered. The night pulsed round him. The yellow light was all over his clothes, mixed with the red. He was like a playing card. A diamond.

Christ Almighty, what was happening to him? His whole body was shaking. He couldn't control himself. He was the king of diamonds, glittering in the cold night.

The packet with the short stories came from Miss Gillespie with a brief note. She hoped that the reading of them would not be a chore. They were in fact a chore. There was nothing new or really creative in any of them. Many were of the standard that he had encountered from classes in school, written beside a radiator on a cold winter's morning. It was not easy to be a good writer. Was he himself a good writer? He pondered on that in the frosty autumn day. His work had appeared in a number of magazines. There had been a certain amount of notice taken of it. But all that he had written he had been in control of. None of it was hallucinatory, primitive, powerful. Much of it was orderly, metrical. He had never had time to work at it. But then again if

137

he did work at it, would it be better? Chaucer had held down a job: so had many other poets.

He was brought face to face with the problem. Had he asked too much of his wife in support of a minor talent? It was an important question. He certainly didn't believe that good poetry should justify human suffering. There had been many times when he had walked into a small draughty hall to find six people gathered to listen to him. Most had never heard of him. Should he perhaps read professionally or should he show himself as the truly vulnerable person who had created the poems? Was that really how the poet gained over the actor in reading? Was this small man with the crushed hat the one who had really created these poems?

In the frosty autumn he thought about that question. Responsibility for the human being. Was a poem greater than a human being? How could he justify the sacrifices his wife had made? After all, she had not married the artist: she had married the human being. Perhaps he had killed her, had caused her cancer.

He had strange ideas about the tenement too. He thought of it as composed of cells instead of rooms. These cells were continually interchangeable. New blood flowed in, old blood flowed out. His wife, too, had lived in a cell, an outlaw one. It had rebelled against the other cells, was determined to destroy them: her whole body was a tenement. Cancer above all was a psychological disease. Her wanderings had been converted into the wanderings of cancer. Maybe he was as much to blame as Cameron. Maybe he had beaten his wife to the ground, to the final bed. He hadn't physically assaulted her, but perhaps he had mentally done so. Perhaps he had done the same to his son who had turned into a human calculator. His selfishness was just as bad as that of the stair-woman's son.

"He now wants to leave the university," she told Trevor. "He says the digs are too expensive, and anyway he doesn't like the landlady. He wants more money from me, but I don't have any to give. 'You get a good degree, you'll get a good job,' I tell him.

'Who told you that?' he said. And of course that's true, to a certain extent. 'Why don't we have a car?' he asks. He doesn't mind me being a stair-lady. He seems to think that this a fine thing. He wouldn't like me to be a teacher. That would be too middle class, he says."

Robin, on the other hand had turned into a bourgeois. He himself was the poet who was supposed to regenerate the dead cells and he had instead created an aluminium mineral bourgeois. He had made his son into a shining middle class paragon. And all because he, the poet, had no real feeling. He had believed that poetry shouldn't show feeling in that sense. What was wrong with these stories that he had been reading was that they showed too much feeling: the feelings spilled over without discipline. The writers were exactly the kind of people who would weep for the characters in a film, in a book. Julia had often told him that he had no real feelings. If he had, he would have done something about Cameron a long time ago. Cameron showed feeling: perhaps Cameron was really a better person than he was himself. Who knew what selfishness really was?

Frosty autumn, his favourite season, burned down to its dregs. And all he could think of was an elegy for his wife. He had never really known her: that was a fact. He hadn't known what she had been doing when he was teaching. She had never told him. She hadn't trusted him. Why are you spending money on that old man, he might have asked. How are you disordering my life which must be kept static, so that I can work properly? Each poem, he now saw, was a loss of blood from his wife's body.

Sometimes he would stand at the door and watch the stair-woman at her cleaning. She was as meticulous as himself. She stayed for the hour that he paid her, and wouldn't leave till the hour was over. You can go now, he would say, but no, she wouldn't go. Her time wasn't complete.

In school he had seen a vision of the future. The pupils no longer wanted to work. Work was no longer an ideal. Idleness was the ideal. Work was unpleasant, and idleness was pleasant. They would not tackle anything demanding. They did not feel in literature the resonance he did. He was an antiquarian, and he had refused to see it. He was a dinosaur who couldn't change: what was needed now was not scholars but human beings. In the past there had been teachers who transmitted a culture to those who came after. But now there was no culture to transmit. Everyone lived in the present. He hadn't seen that. He had worked hard while destroying his wife. Sometimes he wouldn't even take a holiday so that he could carry on with his poetry during the school vacation. And even when he did go on holiday, he was writing, sometimes in the open air. He took a writing pad with him all the time and a pen. No, he wasn't a great poet, it was probably true that he wasn't a good poet. He had perhaps taken up poetry because he had read poetry books.

He stared out at the autumn day. Why did his wife have to be dead before he could see what was wrong with him? He had tried to write about her, but couldn't think of anything to say. Certainly he had feelings now, but couldn't transform them into art. Once he saw her putting stamps into a book. They happened to be Greek stamps and had black profiles on them. Perhaps, he thought, that could be Antigone, Agamemnon. But no, she hadn't thought in that way at all, she patiently put the stamps into her album. She had lived for the present, in the present. He had lived in the past and sometimes in the future. And in the process the living water had flowed past him.

He had wept for her especially the day that Red Cross woman had come for her clothes. As he handed them over there was a finality about the gesture that almost broke his heart. Someone else would wear those clothes, someone whom he would never know, a perfect stranger. What tragedy! Was that not tragedy?

The tenement sweated, as Julia had done in her pale bed. It looked gaunt and tall, as she had done. Life was shifting, changing continually. It was composed of water, blood, not stone or earth. He must break out of the cell. He must do something about the oak tree, about the Camerons, about so many things. He must become a human being.

IT WAS A celebration for the baby's birth, and John had invited Mrs Floss, Mrs Cameron, Mr Cooper (after some reluctance): he had been unable to contact Mrs Miller.

". . . really odd," Linda was saying to Mr Cooper, "There was no photograph, but John says that I can never work the camera properly." She looked fulfilled, happy, after the birth of the child. John was doing his waiter from a sideboard where there was whisky, vodka, gin, beer; he himself drank beer only.

"Think it was a ghost then?" he grinned at Cooper.

"Well, there *was* a family here called Grant. Mother and son. The son would have been over thirty right enough. He was sixteen when I knew them. Thanks," he said, accepting a whisky.

"Lemonade?" John couldn't resist. He thought taking lemonade with whisky was like taking sugar with porridge. He opened the door to Trevor Porter, who had brought a bottle of whisky. The latter took his hat off and placed it on a hook on the hall-stand.

All had admired the baby: Porter made no move to ask to see it. He felt unsure of himself, not knowing what to say. Mrs Floss and Mrs Cameron had left some money on the cot. So had Cooper. Mrs Cameron looked nervous: she had slipped downstairs from the flat above while her husband was out. She hoped he wouldn't come back early and make trouble. Linda, however, had insisted on inviting her since she had given a present to the baby.

The conversation drifted on to ghosts. No one had ever seen a ghost. Porter didn't believe in them. He talked pompously for a while about the unlikelihood of their existence and then became silent. He could sense that Linda felt uneasy in his presence. In a short while they would begin to talk about teachers: he hoped they wouldn't. Everyone talked about teachers: everyone had been taught. Stories were exaggerated, grew into monstrous legends.

But, no, Mrs Floss told them instead about her trip round the world. She was happy sitting there in her red velvet dress which she had bought especially for the occasion. Mrs Cameron wore a blue blouse which made her face look old, haggard. She was shyer than the rest, unused to company.

"I crossed Canada by plane," said Mrs Floss. "Niagara is really as big as they say it is."

"By plane?" said John. "Why not by bus? I thought you could go by Greyhound."

"You can, but I didn't," said Mrs Floss. "But of all the places I visited the one I would have liked to stay in was New Zealand. Auckland is the most beautiful city I've seen."

"How about it?" said John to Linda. "Hong Kong next year, eh? After we've paid the rates and the TV."

Cooper was still thinking about Grant. "A funny boy," he said. "Very fond of his mother. She would put him to his bed if he was tired. He was hardly ever out of his bed."

The baby slept. According to Linda, it was very good, never gave them any trouble.

She felt that he was bright, would grow up to be intelligent. She was sorry for Mrs Cameron, for Mrs Floss, even for Cooper, though he always looked at her legs when she was bending down for the coal. John passed the drink round. Cooper drank a lot, his face reddening like flame. He told Mrs Floss he had a brother in America and was thinking of visiting him. "I haven't seen him for thirty years. Last time he was home he thought we still went round in carts. I have to send him Scottish calendars every year: I don't know what he does with them. Sells them to his friends maybe."

Mrs Cameron said, "They never forget their home, do they?" She had no one abroad. She hadn't been abroad herself. She couldn't talk to Mrs Floss, envied her. Mrs Floss had been everywhere, looked confident, assured.

"I went to the White House too," said Mrs Floss. "I stayed in Washington at the time. Hotels in America are expensive. You don't get your breakfast in them."

"Where do you get your breakfast?" said John.

"Oh, you find a restaurant in the morning." He too had never been abroad. Even old Cooper had been abroad, had served in the war.

"When I was in Africa," he said on cue, "during the war, I saw an Italian soldier lying in the desert. I was alone and he was lying there dead. I bent down. He had a photograph of his family in a wallet. Very strange, I thought, what is he doing here? What am I doing here? I told Marconi about it." (Referring to the owner of the cafe near them.) "Very musical people, the Italians, but not good soldiers."

"They're good at playing the spaghetti," said John laughing. "They put it over their shoulder like bagpipes. Hey, want a tune on my spaghetti? What do you think of that, Mrs Floss?" Mrs Floss laughed and held out her glass for another gin. John couldn't drink gin at all: he thought it was like perfume.

Porter suddenly said, "I can only drink whisky myself." They looked at him. He writes poetry, John would say to Linda. He could only remember from school a poem about a skylark and another one about a blacksmith. He had preferred Mrs Porter to her husband: so had Linda.

"Whisky is the best drink," said Cooper. "The Irish call it a paddy. Did you know that? Whisky's the healthiest drink you can get. They say that people who drink whisky are healthier than people who don't. You should take a nip before you go to bed at night," he said wickedly to Mrs Floss.

"My husband used to drink it," she said. "I never drink it. I drink gin."

"And very nice too," said John, filling her glass. The sooner everybody got drunk the better. Porter reminded him of a teacher he had once had: you never felt easy in his presence. "Boy," he would say, "you should take up woodwork. It would suit your head." He didn't know what to make of Porter, what

subject would interest him. He sat there with his glass in his
hand as if warming himself at a fire. Funny little man with that
hat he wore summer and winter. He wondered if he wore it to
bed. When the roof was being repaired, he, John, had
volunteered to climb up and see that it had been done properly.
Porter had stared at him in amazement.

"You mean, you would go up there?"

"Why not?"

"Well, it's pretty high."

"So is rotten meat," John had laughed.

"Hey, Mrs Cameron, you're not drinking," he said. "Orange
juice then? We've got everything. I'm doing my waiter okay?"
he said to Linda.

Linda laughed. Mrs Cameron took some orange juice.
Suddenly he thought, that would suit her husband all right.
Orange juice. The UDA bastard, the poor woman looks
frightened out of her wits.

"Haven't heard anything of Mrs Miller recently," said Mr
Cooper. "Is she okay?" No one else had seen much of her either.
"She looks very pale," said Linda. "She's growing older."

"A lovely woman that, when she was young," said Cooper.
"Half the town was after her. But she would have nothing to do
with them. Her family should take her away from here and look
after her. One of these days she's going to drop dead in the
street."

"She's getting queer," said Mrs Floss. "One day I heard her
shouting at a policeman, out of the window."

"What for?" said Mrs Cameron, shyly.

"I don't know. Some people grow queer as they become
old."

"That's right," said Cooper. "There was a queer woman who
lived here years ago. She thought if you waved your arms you
were talking about her. Maybe that was what Mrs Miller
thought. The policeman would be waving his arms."

"That's right," said Mrs Floss, "he was directing the traffic. I
knew a woman once and she grilled a slipper. I think she must

have thought it was bacon. Some people shouldn't be left on their own."

"Old age is an awful thing," said John, slapping Linda playfully on the back. They all laughed. "When I'm eighty I'll pee out of the window on to the passers by."

Suddenly Porter said to Mrs Floss, "My wife used to take coffee with you, didn't she?"

"That's right. She was a fine woman. Many a coffee we had together. Every morning at eleven o'clock. I miss her. She used to come after she had finished brushing the stairs."

"Just like the matron used to do," said Cooper, gazing meditatively into his glass. "Of course all these matrons, all these people who work in hospitals, they're very particular. And they often have bad backs from lifting people. Surprising the number of them have bad backs."

"That's right," said Mrs Cameron. They waited for her to continue, but she said nothing more. She kept glancing at her watch as if she intended leaving.

"I had a friend once," said Porter, "and he came to visit me here. Of course he was a mad poet. He leaned out of the window and he delivered a sermon to the passers by. He asked them if they had been saved. Some of them looked up at him, in amazement. Others thought he was quite reasonable." Everyone laughed, except for Mrs Cameron who was remembering her own father.

Porter wanted to tell them some more stories about his "mad" friends, but felt that they wouldn't like them. Some of his friends were nice, some were not. There was one he didn't like, one who in fact had a thin moustache rather like John's. He was an expert on Scottish dialect and was inclined to become intellectually cruel when he was drunk. "Nobody likes me," he once said to Trevor, weeping. He was always drunk, always borrowing money, arriving at people's houses at four in the morning. He was what Trevor would have called a tramp. "I'll send you the money," he would say to him, after he had borrowed it, but he never did. Why was he thinking of him now? Perhaps it was

John's moustache that had brought him to mind. Some of his friends weren't pleasant people really. Egotists. Compulsive talkers about their own subjects, like that man about Scottish dialects. Who apart from himself cared?

". . . a fine fellow her husband." Cooper was still talking about Mrs Miller. "He was burnt, you know. He was repairing a telephone line. And lightning hit him. Funny thing that."

Crucified up there, thought Porter, turning blue. Hung on the wire. Mrs Cameron thought of a sick joke of her husband's. What was Christ doing at Easter? Answer: hanging around. She felt suddenly sick and went to the bathroom. There was a window glowing with colour, a stained glass window.

"What do you think of it," said Linda, who had followed her to see if she was all right. "It's just paper you know. I got it in a supermarket in Glasgow. I thought it would be nice." The window glowed and burned with its reds and greens.

"It's beautiful," said Mrs Cameron, though she was obscurely troubled by it. "Some people are so clever." She had never been clever herself. She had always been clumsy.

If she had been clever she would have taken a job. But she had been too nervous to. She sweated.

When she and Linda went back, Cooper was saying . . . "In the old days rich women used to have companions. You should have a companion," he said to Mrs Floss.

"Shut up, you oaf," said Mrs Floss good-naturedly.

"Why not? Mrs Cameron could be your companion. She could bring you your gin in the mornings."

"If I was rich I would have a companion," Cooper went on, unabashed. He suddenly looked tired and clownish in spite of his jolly red face which burned among them.

"I've got a companion already," said John, handing round more drink.

"He's my companion," said Linda comfortably. John felt happy being the host to all these people. They weren't too bad really. Except that Mrs Cameron was glancing continually at her watch which hung loosely round her thin wrist.

146

Suddenly Porter put his hand in his wallet and said, "I forgot." He took out a pound and gave it awkwardly to Linda. "For the baby," he said. Linda thanked him. Nobody could say he was mean, apart from Robin.

"You mean old bastard," Robin would say. And then Robin himself had become mean. When he came to visit he never brought anything, not even a cake. Could one be a poet and be mean? Most poets he had ever heard of had been prodigal with their personalities, with their possessions. They had poured their gifts on to the world. Mrs Floss wasn't mean, one couldn't say that about her. A lot of the people he knew were mean, mean in their minds, borrowing money all the time as if the world owed them a living. These artistic types whom he had once admired so much: he didn't admire them now at all.

The first poem he had ever had accepted—he had been invited to meet the editor of the relevant magazine in Glasgow. He thought it would be a big house with fine trees around it. Actually it had been a flat with a pub opposite it. There was a small room with poems scattered all over it. He remembered the editor as a bald serious man who had tried to impress him by making his five-year-old recite a section of 'Lycidas'. The boy stared straight in front of him, as if he was reciting a lesson. Poets were poor, their houses were poor. They never had any money. They lived from hand to mouth, they weren't gods.

Linda was passing round sausage rolls, sandwiches, small cakes. He bit at one of them absently and swallowed some whisky after it. One night he had been drinking heavily when he had fallen from a chair. He had been having an argument with another poet, no, it wasn't another poet, it was a headmaster. This headmaster had been in the habit of phoning round to teachers late at night to come and talk to them at his house: he was an insomniac. He was big, bearish, and arrogant. He held court till the early hours of the morning. He used his power arbitrarily and summoned teachers, who came to him even though their wives weren't happy about it. That night he, Trevor, had fallen from his chair. What a humiliation. He couldn't even hold his drink. That had been in England somewhere. He hadn't liked that headmaster sitting in his chair like a king on a throne. Sleeplessly.

". . . I'm not keen on religion myself," Cooper was saying to Mrs Cameron. "I never go to church. Used to, but not now. You should never argue about religion, I always say. I heard a story about a Free Church minister once. When Christ came down to earth, he said, there was no vacancy in the trinity. And this fellow in the congregation said to me, 'Please sir, can I apply for the vacancy in the trinity?'"

They shouldn't laugh about the church, thought Mrs Cameron. She remembered men in black coats, black hats. They were definite, single-minded. A young minister she heard of had hit his wife and they had put him out of the church. But you could never tell who was responsible, the wife or the husband. In this case it was the wife, but they had expelled him just the same. As a matter of fact the wife had been demanding new furniture, a washing machine, all the latest gadgets, and he couldn't afford them. He was a holy man too. He had died of cancer six years after the divorce, and there had been three hundred people at his funeral. He had entered the church late: before that he had been a merchant seaman. His wife was now in England and had a job.

She wished that she could talk as freely as Cooper. The fact was that she never had any opportunity for mixing in company. How could she? And she had always been shy. She could talk to people individually, but not in company. And yet if it wasn't for her husband she would enjoy listening to the conversation. Linda looked so happy, and so did John. They were both so young, the world was ahead of them.

"I think," she said, making a movement to go, "I've left food in the . . ."

"Not at all," said John. "Stay where you are. The night is yet young."

"Oh God, don't let us have a singsong," thought Trevor. "Amazing Grace, Danny Boy, The Wild Rover . . . I've heard them so often at a certain stage in the evening." Amazing Grace would be more like it. He imagined someone sitting at the head of a table and the wife saying "Why don't you say your Amazing Grace?" God waited and listened. Perhaps he only listened sporadically. Even God must get bored sometimes.

". . . had a terrible time once when I was on a boat," Mrs Floss was saying. "Everybody was sick. Glasses were sliding down the table. I got to my feet and went flying through the doors, swing doors they were. I landed on the deck and my handbag skidded all over the place. The ship was going down, I thought, and I was sure it wouldn't come up again. I thought to myself, I'm not a good woman. I haven't been a good woman. What will happen if I drown now? The waves were all grey. But it was too late, you see." She was becoming maudlin now. "The toilet was slippery with sickness. Babies were being sick too." Her face was reddening like Cooper's. Soon she would weep into her gin. John placed a small table in front of her so that she could lay her glass on it. She looked up at him, "You're a pal," she said. "I remember when I was young my father, who was working in the fields, sent me to bring a drink to the harvesters" (she had difficulty in pronouncing 'harvesters'). "My brother was sitting on a bicycle at the gate. He laughed at me when he saw me with the pail. And I threw the pail of water all over him. He started crying and I ran away and hid behind some trees. I stayed there for three hours. And then I heard my father looking for me, and he found me, and he said, 'You'll be all right, Glenda, I promise you. I'll fix it with your mother.' And so I came out. My mother used to hit me with a broom and my brother was her favourite. She didn't listen to my father, and hit me just the same. My brother was brighter than me. He became an accountant, though he wanted to be a violinist." She relapsed into silence.

"Oh, he played the fiddle," said Cooper laughing like a horse. "He fiddled the accounts. These two people ran away with two violins, and do you know what the charge was? Robbery, with violins."

"A pun," thought Trevor, "not a very good joke."

"You know something," he said, "I was never a good teacher. Oh, I knew my subject all right. Perhaps too well. But I didn't like the pupils. That's the thing, you're not teaching a subject, you're teaching pupils. I remember once, this girl whose work I admired, came to see me. 'Please sir, I cannot finish my thesis,' she said. 'What,' I said, 'you come to tell me that after half the year's gone? Why didn't you do it? I'm ashamed of you.' 'I couldn't do it,' she said, and she burst out crying. And I was very angry. You see, I thought she had done something to me, I took the fact that she couldn't finish the thesis as a personal insult." They were all looking at him. Mrs Floss didn't know what he was talking about, but the rest were impressed by the authenticity of his statement. It was as if drink was the Protestant's confessional. For the first time he felt that he was losing his aloofness.

"That's right," said John. "I understand you. I was once, well, I used to like reading Science Fiction, and this day Linda and I were in Glasgow. And I came to this shop where I saw some second-hand science fiction books and others. When I went into the shop the man got up and he said, 'Plenty of books here. Three hundred of the best here. At reasonable prices. Over three hundred. You won't get better bargains anywhere.' So I wandered around looking at the shelves. Only the books were overpriced, for second-hand books. Normally I paid thirty pence at the most for a second-hand paper book, but he was asking seventy pence and more. And he kept following me about. 'Cheap as you can get,' he kept saying, showing me the books and pointing out some special ones. 'Good reading there,' he said. He was a big fellow and I thought there was something wrong with him. He was eating an ice cream cone: it was a hot day. Anyway, I didn't buy any of his books and he followed me outside, and he shouted, 'You think you know about books. But I can tell you don't know anything about them.' I thought he was going to attack me. He was foaming at the mouth. 'I could teach you a thing or two about books,' he kept shouting. And he shook his fist at me. Funny guy."

"I often think," said Porter eagerly . . . "Do you think if you go into a shop and you don't buy anything that the owner of the shop takes it personally?" But this time he felt that he had gone too far. The audience was not interested in a philosophical discussion, in close analysis.

The tenement had grown suddenly silent as if the passers-by had all gone home. "Do you hear the creakings at night in the tenement?" said Mrs Floss suddenly. "You can hear the wood creaking. You never hear it in a new flat."

"That's the wood contracting and expanding with the heat," said Cooper magisterially. "That's what it is."

"Every night I hear it. And cracks. I hear cracks like guns going off. From the sideboard I hear them. About an hour after I put the TV on."

"It must be Little and Large," said John. "No, I tell you it's that woman" (and he named a Scottish singer he disliked). The Ghoul, he called her. "Listen," he would say to Linda. "The Ghoul's on again." When she sang opera he told Linda that she had constipation.

"I didn't know you liked Science Fiction," said Trevor to John. "I used to read Science Fiction. I've got some books in the house. Mostly Sturgeon. You can have them if you like."

"Ta," said John. "Ta very much."

"You'll never get his nose out of a book," said Linda proudly.

I used to read romances, thought Mrs Cameron, nurses and doctors in hospitals, squires and maidens. How long ago that must have been. Many of them were also set in Greece. There was one she specially remembered about a blind girl who had been haunted by her former lover whom she supposed dead. Devil worship; reincarnation it was. And it turned out that she was the reincarnation of a sixteenth century girl and he the reincarnation of a lord who had lived in a castle and had been a devil worshipper.

"They have no open-air toilets in Yugoslavia," Mrs Floss was saying to Cooper. "You have to go to a restaurant. And the same in Italy."

"No open-air toilets?" said Cooper incredulously. "I wouldn't like that. No job for me, eh John."

"How are you liking your job, then?"

"Great. A man came in the other day and he said to me, 'It's too hot out there, I came in for the cool.' Fellow from England he was, with a moustache. And he wouldn't go out because it was too hot. 'Can't stand the heat,' he told me, 'ever since my operation.' He told me that even in the winter time he went about in shirt sleeves. Sweat pouring off him. You never saw anything like it. 'You can stay here,' I told him, 'you can wash your face if you like. Use the facilities.' And we had a great blether. Turned out he was from the Potteries. He took a professional interest in lavatory pans. But he made mostly vases, he told me. And before that he used to work in a glass factory. He didn't like Leeds or Liverpool, but he liked Sheffield and Manchester. Great architecture in Manchester, he told me. That was his hobby, you see, studying architecture. Liverpool, that's a dangerous place, he said. Went to a pub there one night for a beer and I could feel the danger, know what I mean he said."

He's not home yet, thought Mrs Cameron, that must mean he's really drunk. And she was frightened. Please let me get up the stairs before he gets home. But she was afraid to excuse herself to the company, she was so shy.

"This Italian was sitting there. Upright against a rock," Cooper was saying. "You'd have thought he was asleep. They said Italians were cowards and so they were. Interested in music and ice cream. It was very quiet. You could hear the flies. They were moving about his face, hundreds of them. It was very hot. I took his wallet out, and there were these photographs. Fat wife. They say Italians like them fat." He licked his lips, "I could show you that photograph. I showed it to my wife once. Nice woman that, I said to her. Bit of flesh on her." He stopped and then continued as if he hadn't changed the subject at all.

"This policewoman came and it was late at night. She was all right when I left her, I told her. I'll be back, I said to the surgeon.

Simpson it was, he goes to Saudi Arabia for six months in the year. But this policewoman came to the door. It was very cold. It was just after Christmas. You'll be home for the New Year, I told her. But she wasn't." And his eyes filled with tears. He accepted the drink John gave him. "They should have known at the hospital," he said.

"Do you remember that spastic woman who was nearly raped here?" he asked. They remembered.

"Well, the woman she was visiting never speaks to her now. Keep away from my house, she told her. She acts as if the spastic was a prostitute or something. And when the policeman went to see her, she said, I know nothing about it. I heard nothing. I don't want anything to do with her. She's a bad woman. And she slammed the door in his face. Would you believe it? So she's got nowhere to go now. It was the only house she visited, you see. Sometimes I think about that bloke who nearly raped her. But what could I do? I heard the scream, I had to do something, didn't I?" There was self-congratulation in his voice. "But if he'd tried anything on me I'd have fixed him. I've got friends. I'm not worried. He had a scar on his face. Disgusting bugger." And he swallowed more whisky.

Cameron made his way up the road staggering and singing. After a while he stopped and his face became set and angry. He had heard from Mrs Miller, with whom he had had a drink at the station buffet, that his wife was visiting the Masons. She herself had avoided the party as she had no intention of celebrating the birth of a child: she considered the Masons lucky and herself unlucky. Linda Mason had her husband beside her: she had lost hers when not much older than Linda. She raised her glass mockingly to Cameron as she told him about his wife.

Cameron could hardly believe that Greta would have the impudence, the nerve, to visit the Masons and to do it moreover behind his back. If she was doing so now, then she must have had contact with them before. Perhaps she had given the Fenian baby a present, she who had herself remained childless, infertile, barren. He would drag her from that house and hammer her: he looked forward to the night with satisfaction. The aggression surged in him clearly: he had his honest pretext. Mrs Miller's mocking burning face shone in front of him.

When he arrived outside the close, he stood for a moment, swaying and considering. Perhaps what he should do was smash the window which fronted the street. But no, better would be to open the door and see the expression on his wife's face. He stood there and breathed in and out for a while, preparing himself. He closed his big red fist. He could taste the moment inside his mouth. Now they were all happy in there. Then in a short while there would be din, noise, confusion. He had every right to drag his wife out of there: she had betrayed him. He went out into the wind and rain and earned money for her: and she associated with Fenians, his mortal enemies. He thought perhaps he should go upstairs and put on his blue finery, but that would be a waste of valuable time. He banged on the door, shouting, "Come out of there, you Fenian bastards."

There was a sudden silence as if those inside were stunned. He basked in it for a moment. Then the door opened and John Mason was standing in front of him.

"You've wakened the baby," said John. His face was white and set. His whole body was trembling.

"My wife, you've got my wife in there. Send her out here or I'll go in myself," said Cameron. He kicked the door with his boot. He was glad he had wakened the baby.

"You've got twenty seconds to get out of here," said John trembling more than ever. "That's all you've got."

"What do you f...ing mean? I want my wife sent out, you Fenian bastard."

Mason looked down at the door on which Cameron's boot had left a scar. It was as if he could hardly believe what had happened.

"Look," he said, "you've wakened the baby. I've given you your chance. You're an old man. Go up the stair quietly."

"Listen, you Fenian bastard. Tell your Fenian wife to send my wife out or . . ."

Before he could say any more John's head thrust forward and butted him in the face, from which blood suddenly poured. Then John punched him in the stomach. As he fell he kicked him viciously. He had gone berserk with rage.

"John, stop it," screamed Linda behind him.

"Stop it," shouted Greta Cameron, rushing out to see her husband lying on the stone. She beat on John's body with her small fists. After a long while he heard voices which seemed at first to come from a distance, then closer. He drew a deep breath and stood there silently. There was blood on his shoe.

"You . . . you ruffian," Greta Cameron was shouting, "You've killed him." There was blood on Cameron's face and head, but he was breathing. His wife bent down to touch his forehead. She swayed and seemed about to faint.

"Bastard," John was saying over and over.

Trevor Porter gazed down at Cameron, feeling sick. His mind was in a turmoil of emotions. On the one hand he was glad that Cameron was lying there like a felled oak. On the other, he was frightened by the violent battering that John had inflicted on him. Inside the house the baby was crying. Linda ran in, leaving the others at the door.

As Trevor stood there, he thought of his wife, and Cameron's body stretched in front of him reminded him of her. He even felt a curious pity for Cameron: he suddenly looked old and empty, not at all terrifying. John had been much fitter when the time came, much more aggressive.

Mrs Floss said to him, "He deserved it." Her face was shaking with excitement. "He should never hit a woman." John leaned down as if he were a doctor inspecting a patient and said to Cameron, who perhaps was not even hearing him, "Don't ever touch my door again or I'll give you another doing. I'm not your wife. I hope you're listening, you fat bastard."

Cameron lay there almost posthumously in the silence.

Then John said, "We'd better take him upstairs. Will you

help me?'' he asked Trevor and Cooper, who had been gazing at the fight with a mixture of amazement and satisfaction. He seemed to have forgotten his army days or perhaps he saw in Cameron the Italian he had watched so carefully in the desert.

"You watch what you're doing. Be careful," Mrs Cameron was shouting as they lifted him up, bumping into the wall with its green scarred paint, as they climbed the stair.

"The door's open," Mrs Cameron was saying. They made their way through the flat as if they were carrying a corpse and laid Cameron on a bed. His wife immediately dashed to the kitchen to put the kettle on. Then she came in.

"Out of my house," she shouted to John, "hitting an old man like that and not fighting fair. Out." She pursued them till they were on the stair again. They walked down the stone steps in silence.

"We're witnesses," said Cooper eagerly. "It was him or you. We saw it." He glanced worshipfully at John.

"What if she sends for the police?" said John.

"She won't send for the police," said Trevor definitely.

"Why not?"

"I just know. She won't have anything to do with the police."

"Bastard," said John, "waking the baby. He's an animal. Want to come in for a cup of coffee?"

"No thanks," said both Trevor and Cooper. "It's after eleven."

"Okay then." John suddenly felt the responsibility of a family. Out there he had been defending it. He and Cameron were quite like each other, thought Trevor, one defending, the other attacking. He looked around him. For the first time he saw the tenement clearly as old and crumbling. There were white patches on the ceiling upstairs. As they descended they met Mrs Miller toiling upstairs, clutching the bannister. She was obviously drunk. A rancid smell came from her fur coat.

"Good evening," said Trevor, forgetting that it was later than that. She didn't answer. For a moment he felt an immense pity for her returning to her empty unlighted flat. They heard her trying to fit her key into the lock and then she suddenly shouted, "F . . k off the lot of you."

Defiantly she stood there at the door, staring down at them, her face palely powdered. She was indomitable, masterful. In a strange way Trevor couldn't but admire her. "Silly old trout," said Cooper. They continued their descent.

Trevor stopped at his own door. "Good night," he said to John. "You had to do what you did. He won't tamper with you again. He won't live it down. He looked just like an exploded balloon. Maybe you've done some good."

"I don't know," said John, "You never know with people like that."

"She should leave him," Cooper insisted eagerly. "She should move in with Mrs Floss. I wasn't joking."

"Good night, then," said Trevor. He opened and shut the door behind him. He switched on the light in the lobby.

The house was large and quiet. All he could hear was the thin crying of a baby from below. He made himself some coffee and as he did so, he thought of Julia. Funny how when he had seen Cameron lying there – all that he longed for – the outstretched body seemed an anti-climax, and the battering not sufficient for the pain that he had inflicted on himself and his wife. Not at all an equal exchange for these long nights of fear, frustration and anguish. How suddenly old and fat and out of condition Cameron had looked. And what viciousness he had seen in John's revelation of aggression. He shouldn't have hit the man's head with his boot. But at the same time he had been defending his family, as Trevor had not done. When Cameron had burst in like that he himself had stood up, sublime in his drunkenness, and would have fought him, but John had forestalled him. Or he believed that he would have fought him.

He stood by the cooker in the quiet of the night. Upstairs, Mrs Cameron would be wiping her husband's head and face free of the blood. He was all she had, her child. Tomorrow perhaps, she would make friends with John and Linda again, or she wouldn't speak to them. One never knew the ways of women. How deep love, if love it was, went. She too had seen her conquering hero lying outstretched on the stone.

Trevor sipped his coffee slowly. The tenement was so old. It had seen so much: this was only one incident in its tangled history. The door was scarred and losing its paint. The bins overflowed with rubbish. The walls were flaking and so was the ceiling. It was a place for derelicts, though once it had been fresh and fine.

He prowled restlessly about the flat, from room to room. They suddenly seemed alien. It was as if Julia had been placated by that violence which had created a peace in his own mind. How curiously peaceful he felt. "Rest in peace," he said under his breath. "You can leave this place now, both of us can leave. This will be our last shift, I promise you."

He gazed across at the church, the graveyard, shining in the moonlight. The street was quiet as if exhausted after a death or a birth. The graves had a yellow shine. This tenement was finished. He knew that the Masons would shortly leave, if they could. They couldn't afford to have Cameron near them. There would only be left Mrs Floss, and himself, and Cooper, and Mrs Miller, and the Camerons, and he didn't want to stay.

He said goodbye to the tenement in that yellow light which irradiated the walls. The silence was now so deep that he thought he could hear as far as the end of the world. He was like a flower in a vase, peaceful.

He went into the bedroom and removed his clothes. Some of Julia's things were still lying on the sideboard. He listened carefully. There was a new noise. It was the noise of water flowing; another pipe must have burst. The roof, and now a burst pipe. He could hear the noise brimming below the kitchen window. There would be a squabble as to who would pay for its repair. The water was loud in the night.

He lay in his bed staring up at the ceiling. Lights from passing cars made transient crosses on it, scissoring each other. He heard above him the restless steps of Mrs Cameron as she tended her husband. The baby had ceased to cry. There was a time when one had to leave, when nothing more could be done. A line for a poem sprang into his mind.

In the time of the useless pity he turned away . . .

He must move out of the middle of the dark wood, out of the waste of rusty wheezing pipes, unfinished roofs. He deserved better than this, didn't he?

"Didn't he?" he asked Julia.

She didn't answer, but in the middle of the peace, he was not unreassured. The moon lay gently on her bottles of powder and scent, on her finally discarded things.

I will leave here, he said aloud. I will begin again. And the words did not sound strange or impossible. I will sell this old flat and buy a new one, a smaller one. Perhaps not even in this town. He was tired of sick pipes, flaking paint, a whole body disintegrating. The use of the tenement was over. It was time to leave it.

The noise of the burst pipe was a torrent in the night.